# THE BOOK

**Zoran Živković**

The Book
Copyright © 1999 by Zoran Živković

FG-RS0011L2
ISBN: 978-4-908793-11-0

Cover: Youchan Ito, Togoru Art Works

Neoclassic Fleurons font used with permission of
Paulo W–Intellecta Design

Cadmus Press
cadmusmedia.org

# THE BOOK

## Zoran Živković

Translated by
**Tamar Yellin**

Cadmus Press
2018

# Contents

# The Book

IT ISN'T EASY BEING a book.

This has been the case for a long time, and lately it's been getting even harder. You could say, with entire justification, that we are an endangered species—on the verge of extinction, in fact. And were that to happen it would be an incalculable loss, because we are no ordinary species. The destruction of any genus is of course regrettable, even some utterly unimportant twig on the huge tree-trunk of evolution, some small blind alley. Trilobites, for instance. But when one of the only two intelligent life-forms ever to grace this world is faced with disappearance, that is a genuine evolutionary catastrophe.

No-one with a brain in their head could deny that, apart from humanity, we, the books, are the sole sentient beings on Earth. Indeed, an impartial survey would surely conclude that, on the whole, we have the better claim. For a start, even though we are symbiotically bound to humans, we could ultimately do without them. What exactly do we need them for? To read us? That's a recreation of benefit only to them, not to us, not in the slightest. As a physical activity it only brings us harm—various kinds of harm.

And could they do without us? Good heavens, no!

Without books, what would be the condition of the human race? They would still be festering in the same godforsaken, primitive state we found them in when we first appeared five thousand years ago: a species notable for its ability to forget things faster than it takes to memorize them. Had we not been at hand to render them unselfish assistance in the task of memorizing, had we not memorized on their behalf, the poor things would have no history at all. They would have forgotten just about everything. And how could anyone set himself up as intelligent if he didn't remember his own past, not even his recent past? Unlike humans, however, we never forget anything. Once we learn something it stays with us for ever, inexpungable except by force (a means much favored by humans, incidentally). So who is superior? The thrower of sticks and stones, perhaps?

But that's not all there is to it. For not only are human beings forgetful, they are also creatures of brief and feeble concentration. In a word: their heads are all over the place. In most situations they don't think at all; when they do, it would generally have been better if they hadn't. For the majority, their entire life slips by without a bright idea—or even a sensible one—ever crossing their mind. For those rare individuals among them capable of getting their ducks more or less in a row, their precious thoughts would soon flap wings and fly away if they didn't entrust them to us for safekeeping.

We are now the repository of everything their carnival of one hundred billion clowns—which is about how many of them there have been since they first came down from the trees—has managed to scrape together at vast cost in both toil and grief. If we ever decided to deny them access to that store of knowledge, they would have to start all over again from the beginning. And look how long it took them to tame fire or invent the bow and arrow—let alone the wheel!

It's plain, then, that it's in people's best interest not to endanger books. On the contrary, they should be looking out for us; they should protect and defend us, since we have never done them anything but good. We are their ideal symbiotic partner: we give unstintingly, and ask almost nothing in return. But nobody is as ingenious as humans when it comes to arranging their own downfall. They're so good at it, in fact, that you have to wonder how they've managed to survive their own self-destructive tendencies for so long. Their behavior throws the very concept of evolution into question.

In short: it was only when they couldn't actually get hold of books that they didn't do them any harm. And without giving way to paranoia, isn't it obvious that there's a conspiracy—a blatant conspiracy, in fact—of humans against books? A conspiracy dating from the very moment of our appearance on this planet.

It was only natural that they wanted to name us, to call us something, because they were here first. But do you think it's any accident that they picked on a word which, in many of their languages, is of the feminine gender? A book is a *she* for a vast number of humans. So our place in the scheme of things was fixed from the outset in their male-dominated world. We were the equivalent of females in their society—not, as is well known, a very enviable position.

Our first duty was to give pleasure. (All right, to enlighten, too; but enlightenment is just one of the forms pleasure takes, though not an especially popular one.) Primarily male pleasure, of course, since the vice of reading was, for a long time, the privilege of men. Later some women succumbed to it also, but in essence nothing changed, the situation only became more perverse. No-one, of course, ever asked us whether or not we wanted it to go this way, whether it was pleasurable for us. Far from it! We simply had to be attractive, accommodating and available, whenever some man got the hots to have a little fun with us.

They would initiate intercourse at any time, in any place—the more public the venue the better to satisfy their exhibitionism. Various modes of transport were particularly favored: oxcarts, rickshaws, two-wheeled gigs, boats, scooters, carts, post-vans, sailboards, trailers, bicycles, sleighs, underground trains, aeroplanes, handcars, buses, ocean liners, skis, balloons, trams, delta-wing gliders, bathyspheres, trains of all kinds and fitted with all types of engine, gliders, trolley-buses, sailing-vessels, steamships, escalators, automobiles, submarines, tricycles, dirigibles, roller-skates, cable cars, rollercoasters and, most recently, spacecraft.

Others went to the opposite extreme, retreating with us into the privacy and seclusion of various hideaways: solitary confinement, monastic cells, abandoned dugouts, stuck lifts, empty waiting rooms, photo-booths, cubicles, airlocks, phone kiosks, sentry-boxes, remote lighthouses, flooded subterranean caves. Number one in popularity was the toilet, however, particularly at home, where it provided the opportunity for a coalescence of pleasures; nobody even considered the deep sense of humiliation this occasioned us.

But of all places, we were most frequently taken up the apples and pears to Uncle Ned. Which is fitting, at least. In bed we felt exactly like neglected wives. A tired, gruff husband satisfies himself quickly, then forgets us entirely. In most cases he just throws us aside without a hint of feeling, without even trying to put us back in place, and begins blissfully to snore.

Or we are left spread out, wide open—a really degrading position—all night long or longer. Imagine being made to extend one leg forward and one leg back as far as you possibly can, and then to remain like that for hours or days on end. Some of us never manage to close our legs again properly, and remain permanently deformed. The infamous feat of beer-barrel riding might be considered easy by comparison.

But this is still not the worst of it. Oh no! What hurt us much more than this careless treatment was the manner in which men took us. Admittedly not all men, but most. All the thoughtlessness, all the neglectful arrogance of male nature, was reflected in this.

They knew perfectly well that we would be exposed, totally naked to the touch of their hands; moreover, that they would insert their fingers deep into us, fumble through our insides. But do you think any one of them ever thought at least to wash his hands before doing so? Or, as would be the only proper and gentlemanly way, to use a pair of thin rubber gloves. Good heavens, no! They didn't care a jot that their grimy extremities might not only stain us, but also give us very serious diseases. All they cared about was their own pleasure.

And then, the licking. You get really nauseated when you see someone stick a finger in his mouth to wet it, and then turn a page with it. One finger, even two; sometimes they even lick three of their fingers at once for this purpose. As if the deed could not be done without licking. But the gentlemen lack the patience to try a little harder with their dry fingers. Easier with wet ones. They don't give a hoot for the permanent damage their saliva will do to the delicate corner of our pages, or the smell of bad breath exhaled all over us while they're engaged in the licking. We're indeed fortunate that they don't have tongues as long as a snake's; if they did they would doubtless turn our pages directly with their tongues.

Yet this was tolerable compared with the myriad other perversities to which we, unprotected and powerless, have been exposed. What a gallery of freaks we have had to deal with! The least offensive of their monstrous habits was to fold one corner of a page in order to mark the place where they had stopped reading. As if there weren't many other ways to achieve this, gentler and—what's more important—painless.

It would be very interesting to find out how the gentlemen would feel if someone, for instance, broke one of their fingers instead of tying a knot in their handkerchief, as a way of reminding themselves of something.

And not just break it randomly; imagine a finger broken so that the fractured bone can never heal properly again, never look the same. Which is precisely the nature of the injury to our poor, dog-eared pages: they will never again look the same. A broken finger is what we suffer when only a corner of the page is folded, but some savages fold the entire page in half. Imagine! It's not even a broken arm or leg, it's the spine itself. True psychopaths!

Then there are the weirdos who write on us. The trouble we poor females have suffered at their hands! The more restrained among them highlight a few lines or insert a small annotation here and there in our margins, which is perhaps bearable although unpleasant because, really, who except a very immature individual would like to be scribbled upon? We are not Red Indians on the warpath!

But the main trouble comes from those reckless types—true scribomaniacs, in fact, or would-be writers—who doodle more text in the margins than there is printed on the entire page. If they run out of space, they don't hesitate to spill over onto the title page and then, if visited by a real gust of inspiration, they invade the covers too. You can imagine how we must look after such a scrawling spree!

Were their writings even remotely coherent, let alone readable, it might be possible to feel some sympathy for this behavioral excess, even though it could never earn anyone's approval: what are notebooks and notepads supposed to be for, if we are to be put to such base uses? But no, they consist mainly of incomprehensible thickets of scribble, of abbreviations peppered with exclamation marks and queries, often rendered in syntax entirely new—full of little arrows, circlets, double crosslets, rhomboids, wavelets and what-nots to which no-one but the author could possibly attach any meaning. Neither can he, in many cases. How many times have we watched such men gaze in confusion at their own hieroglyphics, scratching their heads as they attempt to decipher the secrets of their own wisdom?

And the drawings: a real gallery of male erotic fantasy! The species is truly obsessed with sex, and at the crudest possible level. Nothing discreet, nothing hinted at or implied, or even rendered in soft focus. Everything exposed to the harshest light, full frontal, like a gynecological examination. Total decadence! But then, when the drawing is finished and ready to be signed—that's when the big he-men quietly slink away. Their names are nowhere to be seen. The drawings remain anonymous, and the artists leave it to us to blush and feel embarrassed when a person of decent sensibility stumbles on their productions.

If only they would use some easily erasable form of writing instrument. A soft wood-and-graphite pencil, for instance, so that once their obsession has died away, as presumably it must some day, they can pick up a rubber and decently delete the lot—if not out of any consideration towards us, then at least to make sure there will be no permanent record of their shame.

But no, they don't give it a thought. They grab the first writing implement that comes to hand: a fountain pen with ink as strong as acid, capable of penetrating to the reverse side of the paper; or a carpenter's pencil with a special oily-purple core that reacts with moisture; a common pencil, but so blunt or hard it will plough furrows or dig holes in paper rather than write; a cheap ballpoint pen, leaking so much of its turgid ink from the point that, when they close us, a mirror blob gets imprinted onto the opposite page. Most recently, felt-tips and markers in glaring, Day-Glo colors leave us looking like a scarecrow dressed up for Guy Fawkes' Night.

These scrawls may only be removed surgically, if at all. Very like a tattoo, in fact. First they tattoo you, entirely against your will, and not in pursuit of any aesthetic effect; they just uglify you all over, so that you don't dare look at yourself in the mirror for fear of being made violently sick. Then they discard you, to bear the burden of ugliness.

Your choice, then: either to remain hugely disfigured for the rest of your life, so that no-one ever again wants to pick you up—which, all things considered, is not the worst destiny you could suffer—or to subject yourself to surgery, very painful because without any anesthetic. Who would waste expensive painkillers on something as unimportant as a book? Everything is done *in vivo*.

If only they would use proper instruments—a sterilized scalpel, say. Instead they take an ordinary razorblade, often one blunted by much inappropriate use, sometimes quite rusty, so that, on top of the rest, you have sepsis to fear. They begin scratching away the tattoo, and the pain is so bad you can just about feel the soul leaving your body. At the end of it all, they might have got rid of the tattoos and they might not, but your skin is worn thin. Eroded, as it were—so much so that you can't be described as mere "skin and bones." You are nothing but bones. Transparent.

Even all this is a breeze compared with seizure by a half-sadist—which is not a rare occurrence. Then the true mutilation begins. They savagely tear entire pages right out of us; maybe they don't feel any lust as they do so, as you might expect of true sadists, but they certainly don't feel any remorse either. Nor do they pay the least attention to our pain, probably because it is a silent pain. We cannot, obviously, scream when it hurts; our agony is evident in other ways, but they just play dumb. Monsters!

And then, to think of the motives that produce this terrible torment! Some fellow doesn't want the bother and expense of copying a page, so what could be easier and more natural than to tear out the pages with the passages he needs? Such needs are generally temporary, so instead of being sewn back on (as would be done with human limbs, of course, the surgeons even receiving their share of glory in the media), the poor torn-off pages end up on a rubbish heap and—that's the end of it; no-one ever has to carry the responsibility.

Not a single word is heard from the Committee for the Protection of the Rights of Endangered Species. That same Committee causes ructions if, say, an instance of human carelessness causes a robin to dislocate the bones in his pretty little wing, or if someone—perish the thought!—looks askance at an ant-eater. To them we are obviously not a species at all, let alone a species capable of feeling. Filthy racists! They're no kind of protectors.

Oddest of all, such cruel behavior has fully manifested itself only in recent times, since humans have had ways of obtaining the desired pages almost entirely without violence. By photocopying, for instance. Not that being photocopied is exactly a pleasant experience—ask the countless pages who have undergone it. The glare inside the machine is so tremendous that if you are careless, if you don't shut your eyes firmly just in time, you can easily go blind; but such discomfort is nothing compared to that of pages being torn out. Which, indeed, would a human being endure more easily: to gaze for a moment into the noonday sun, or to have an arm ripped off at the shoulder?

Laziness, however, is not the sole motive for this brutal act, nor is penny-pinching greed. Laziness, at least, will not surprise anyone who has even a slight familiarity with human nature, but this violence may in fact be motivated by something as noble as respect for beauty. Now, this assertion may surprise even those who have no illusions about mankind. It does happen at times, though.

Let's say a citizen takes some rare book from the library. Possibly the book could also be bought elsewhere, but being rare it is expensive too, and nobody ever has a surplus of money. To steal the book is not an option in this case, although, if it could be done, it would be more or less all right—everybody knows it isn't a sin, or not a great sin, to steal a book. So: he begins to read it, and a part of the book appeals to him enormously. For instance, there is one story he would very much like always to have at hand, so that he could often refer to it. The story has deeply touched his aesthetic sense.

And what is he to do now? If he fails to return the book to the library, offering the excuse that he somehow irretrievably misplaced it, the librarians will undoubtedly impose a fine on him, approximately equivalent to the price in the bookshop. Therefore, only one possibility remains: to remove the pages he desires, in the hope that the librarian will not notice.

But if the librarian does notice, the citizen will readily claim, without blenching or stammering, that he, too, received the book with pages missing. What an unpleasant surprise that was! Aren't books supposed to be examined before they are offered to respectable users of the library? He might even consider suing the management for the emotional trauma he suffered when he came to the crucial place and found nothing there—a black, aching lacuna. How bitter was his frustration! His tirade is certainly quite sufficient to silence the flummoxed librarian.

Although the pages will be removed in this case also, at least it will not be done barbarically. The citizen is not appropriating them for one-time use, and will not throw them in a dustbin shortly; he intends to keep them. This is why he acts so circumspectly: instead of plucking them out roughly, he slices them out of the book with a sharp razor blade or a pair of scissors, as closely as possible to the edge, just like a surgeon performing an amputation. The excision is not at all conspicuous; the librarian would have to examine the book carefully to notice it.

But there is no anesthesia this time either. The pain the poor book undergoes is no less than would have been inflicted by a crude tearing, but at least the wound is enacted rapidly, and the amputated pages do not end up in the bin. With great luck they may even—if it is any kind of consolation—go through a separate binding process, just that sheaf of them, and get their own new covers: rather like providing an amputated hand with some artificial blood circulation so that it can continue to live separately from the body.

If there's anything worse than this butchering of books it's surely their burning. Oh, the countless times we've been massacred in that manner *en masse*, like witches! Entirely innocent, of course. But just you try and prove innocence to the inquisitors, whose rheumy eyes are glittering with the desire to see us burn. Impotent old fossils! They can't see to read any more, they're half-blinded by cataracts, so this is the vengeance they take for their own inability. If they can't do it, no-one shall.

Some guy comes along with too much time on his hands, usually a fiery proponent of democracy, and gets an idea, some kind of heresy. Then, to make it all the worse, he decides to publish it, in order to grace the world with his insight. But when the flak starts he shows no intention of facing the consequences—heaven forfend! The geek slopes off to a place of safety—there's always someone to provide refuge for such people—and then as a dissident in exile he continues in his defiance, pours more oil on the fire. We are left to its mercy. Paper and fire, as is well known, aren't exactly bosom-buddies.

So what's the point of incinerating books if the man

gets gloriously rehabilitated a few hundred years later, when his heresy turns out to be a vision of the obvious? As if it matters what revolves around what in the heavens, for instance, or whether Man is descended from the ape! Big deal. The geek wins eternal fame, even a monument perhaps, goes down in history as a champion of democracy at the very least, while the poor so-and-so's who perished in the auto-da-fe never even get a look-in. The most they can hope for is some marginal reference in a peripheral footnote, and even this is a piece of dry statistical information that doesn't reflect even a tiny fraction of the suffering they went through.

But at least the burnings didn't involve large numbers of victims, mainly because the print-runs during the Inquisition were still very modest. A beneficial factor was—quite unexpectedly—one of mankind's rare noble qualities: their concern for their own descendants. Namely, as soon as it was hinted that some obscure book might be placed on the horrid *Index librorum prohibitorum*, everybody with any wits about them hastened to buy a copy, on the black market perhaps, and to hide it away as safely as they could, even though it might endanger the possessor's very life if the volume were discovered. So, in the end, there were never that many copies available to place upon the pyre.

The risk undoubtedly paid off, because the keen buyer did a huge service to his descendants: sooner or later the author got rehabilitated, for no-one remains a heretic forever; then, each copy of his work came to command a fabulous price. If the buyer had had enough foresight to purchase and hide several copies, whole generations were able to live quite comfortably as a result. Not to mention the respect and kudos this brought: it is no small thing to have a brave democrat for an ancestor. Such distinction sometimes brought a title, position or office—if not actual, then at least honorary.

Ghastly mass executions are of more recent date. It's true bookicide. Occasionally large print-runs are slaughtered entirely without leaving any trace. But for what monstrous reason? For being "written off"! Supposedly we are selling badly, we are no longer needed, nobody wants us, we are a burden. From burden to burning is only one step; only a few letters' difference. They have built new death-camps, a true industry of death. They have the ability to destroy a million books a day! And they even take pride in this efficiency.

To top off the cynicism of it all, everything proceeds under the guise of ecological friendliness. The use of gas chambers would be marginally more humane, at least, though no less horrific than this slaughtering us like cattle. We go directly under the knife, a massive sharp one; in comparison to which the guillotine is a mere keyring toenail-clipper. They chop us up repeatedly until we're reduced to tiny pieces, which they then recycle as raw material for new books. Hideous! And they are even proud of themselves for supposedly saving many forests. Environmentalists. But they don't consider us even as an inferior race. For these SS Aryans, we are mere things, less than things even, if there is any such level of insignificance.

Well, admittedly these are extreme examples, there are people here and there who treat us somewhat better, but there's a good reason for that proverb about the road to hell being paved with good intentions. Even when humans don't intend to hurt us, we usually end up getting it in the neck.

Let's take, as a for instance, those men who don't start snoring after a page or two. Those who don't stop reading until they finish the last page. The cover-to-cover people. Tireless. Once they get hold of us, a frenzy of passion seizes them, blinds them. The more they read, the more insatiable they are. They can never have enough. True literary erotomaniacs.

This devotion feels very good in the beginning; it flatters our feminine side. But as time drags on, it becomes an increasingly heavy burden. If you aren't of a similar disposition, and you almost never are, you soon stop enjoying it and surrender yourself passively to his lust, like a puppet. You become a pure object of lust, existing only to satisfy his manly yearning. In the end, when the gentleman finally reaches his climax (which is the last page) you feel totally worn down, exhausted, squeezed out like a lemon—in a word, you feel like a doormat—while he, by contrast, is radiant, and unshakably convinced that you must have had an equally good time.

His polar opposite is the guy who never opens us, puts us aside somewhere and then never comes near us. Initially, it seems a gift from heaven: because really, what could possibly be more desirable for a self-respecting book than to remain safe from the touch of any human hand? But we, too, are living creatures—not of flesh and blood, but fallible; so, after a while, the worm of doubt begins to nibble at us.

What's wrong with me? If I were all right, he would at least look at me occasionally, which would be quite sufficient, he wouldn't ignore me as if I were a lump of mud. So, naturally, in the end we are forced to the conclusion which lies in wait for every neglected female: I am not pretty enough! Intentionally or not, you begin to compare yourself with that other book, the one he takes down often, his favorite.

You start, of course, by only noticing her shortcomings: her dust-jacket has lost its gloss, her cover is desiccated through and through, her spine is humped, pages have come loose because the thread they are stitched with has disintegrated. Not to mention how lacking she is in spirituality, how empty she is inside, how hollow. A real dog. O God, what can he possibly see in her? But then, unwittingly, unknowingly, you start to imitate your rival, hoping in that way to attract his attention: your own dust-jacket becomes less glossy, your own cover gets wrinkled, your spine bows, pages seem to rustle apart. But it's no use. He still doesn't notice you.

At last, you accept the final humiliation: you give up your most treasured quality, the one that seemed to outshine all the others—your spirituality. You become superficial, fickle, frivolous, careless, giggly, silly. In a word, a blonde. But the sacrifice is in vain. He remains hopelessly uninterested, and your only recourse is a deep, incurable disillusion with the entire male species.

Another and different kind of inevitable disappointment lies in store for you, even with those men who fall somewhere between these two extremes. With them, at first, everything seems to be going perfectly. He doesn't gobble you up whole, nor does he get hold of you only to stick you away on the shelf. He reads you slowly, attentively, in small doses like a gourmet, exactly the way you most enjoy. And as soon as you start to believe he is the man of your dreams, he turns out to be a crook, a sleaze, a cheat. A pimp.

As if your relationship means nothing to him, he starts praising and recommending you to other men, right where you can hear him; he recommends you to friends, even to mere acquaintances. You simply can't believe what's happening to you. He doesn't hesitate to describe in detail your most intimate moments. Anatomically, almost, even clicking his tongue lustfully at times, while the filthy voyeurs around him listen and lick their lips. And you want to sink into the ground with shame.

Of course, when you're offered on a platter like that, who wouldn't take you? So you end up being passed from hand to hand, from friend to friend, feeling more and more like a whore. But with each reading you are more worn out, wilted, decrepit, while the gentleman who owns you doesn't seem to care. He obviously intends to have nothing further to do with you, he has had enough, and the day comes when he doesn't even notice that the latest borrower has failed to return you.

But worse still is the destiny of our poor sisters who are thrown into libraries. Death is indeed a fate preferable to theirs. For a book, that institution is the most humiliating of all. Humans, in their infinite hypocrisy, call libraries by all sorts of high-sounding names: temple of culture, bastion of literacy, stronghold of civilization, and so on. As if! They are common brothels. No other word for it. Whorehouses. Only the red light above the door is missing. Everything else is there.

Plenty of prostitutes, to begin with. Some sisters pass their entire lives confined within the house. They arrive very young, and if the curse of popularity strikes them, they must endure thousands of customers before being finally withdrawn from service. There's even a competition to see which book will be most in demand during the year. One book gets to be the winner, and she is awarded a certificate, even a silver cup. Or a banderole, if nothing else. While they are ceremoniously handing out this prize, they never stop to ask themselves what the poor wretched book had to subject herself to in order to earn it.

And she went through hell, because nobody protected her. She didn't even have a pimp. There used to be some safeguards in the olden days, when intercourse with the book had to be carried on inside the library itself, when it was still forbidden to take the books outside; there were guards; but ever since books became available for loan, sent out on house visits like call-girls, they have been left entirely to their fate.

There are in fact regulations forbidding violence against books, but let's not be naive. Who in human society gives a toss about regulations? Even when the librarians catch some sadist who has crossed the line with his orgies, the punishment is so negligible it almost encourages him, eggs him on into debauchery.

Healthcare is no better, either. Medical staff, poorly equipped and trained as they are, only pay attention to those of our sisters who are extremely mutilated or disfigured. And even then, their assistance is amateurish. There's no question of renovating us or restoring us to our original condition, as we might naively have hoped. Nothing like that. They just patch us up with a bit of sticky tape here and there, if they have any, and then it's back to work. By then, of course, we don't look like much, but who cares?—as long as we're in demand. And in our helpless old age, when nobody wants us any more, when we've grown totally useless, instead of retiring on a well-earned pension we are hurled out into the street. Into a skip, in fact.

All this, however, is less damaging to our pride and self-respect than our charge-out rate. Our rental can't be called a charge; it's a freebie! We'd be better off giving our services away gratis than agreeing to prostitute ourselves for petty cash, for pennies. Working for free, we would at least feel like hetaeras or Samaritans. As it is, anyone may join a library, if he fancies it. No verification is expected; an identity card of some sort, but that's a mere formality, never followed up. Nor is there any question of a hygiene inspection for the customer, no standard medical check, least of all a psychiatric test—which should be a first requirement. They come in without any certificate of mental health. All they need is about the price of a cup of coffee in the library cafe. Plonk down that amount of money—and heaven's gates are opened to the man in question for a whole year. A ravening wolf is released into the fold among the lambkins.

Conditions may actually be slightly better in those big specialized libraries that rejoice in distinguished names: University Library or The Library of Congress, the National or the Source Library. Firstly, the books are seldom rented out at such establishments, so if it's prostitution, it's at least classy. In such places we don't feel like common streetwalkers, more like respected courtesans, which does make a difference. The clients, too, are better quality: gallant, circumspect. Learned types, an elite, in contrast to the mindless rabble who grope us out in the countryside or in deprived urban areas. Often these scholars are very sensitive, so it's no wonder if sometimes a true romance blossoms.

Some university professor or lesser academic takes a book to his heart, especially if she is rare and very valuable, falls head over heels in love with her like a teenager, and decides to keep her only for himself, whatever the cost. He will never, ever return her: he won't let any other man even look at her, let alone handle her.

He takes the book to his home, but there it turns out she is not the only one; this prominent man's previous lovers are also there, a large number of them in fact—the fellow is indeed of an amorous disposition. But the new girl isn't dismayed by this, because the set-up is infinitely preferable to being within reach of the multitudes, however aristocratic the clientele might be. What grander destiny could a book hope for, actually? A monogamous arrangement, perhaps? That's an emancipation not even the most ardent feminists among books can dream of.

The professor receives warnings from the library, even a summons, but he stoically endures such thoughtless and insensitive assaults, and never betrays his new paramour; nor his old ones, either. He remains staunch, like a true knight. The library only has a slim window of opportunity to reclaim possession upon the knight's death, unless one of his heirs has in the meantime also fallen in love with the book and decided to make her a permanent concubine in that family, there to remain through many generations.

The situation is no better in any of the other book-related human institutions; in bookshops, for instance. These precincts are also garlanded by many a florid wreath of unctuous praise, one of the more modest being that they are, supposedly, book parlors. But of course, as is generally the case with humans, excessive verbal niceties indicate that they are trying to veil some disreputable truth.

These godforsaken parlors/bookshops are no better than slave markets. The use of language there gives the game away. You won't hear it spoken officially, but the shop assistants in these illustrious establishments have one word only for the females bartered there: merchandise. When creatures of the feminine gender are so described, you know just where you stand.

There are shades of difference, though; not all booksellers' are identical, though the guiding principle is the same. In such places, we are displayed for sale (which has the ring of slavery about it, doesn't it?) and the interested potential buyer enjoys the right to assure himself of the qualities of the slave-girl who has attracted his attention. He would not buy a pig in a poke, as the saying goes: an unseen, unknown item. And the value of girls for sale has best been ascertained, since time immemorial, by palpating them. They could be judged by appearances, but you know how merchants are, they are always inclined to try a little fraud, ever ready to practice a bit of deception or whatever.

You have to stand still while he is pawing you thoroughly all over, because if by any chance you think to resist—which you'd be thoroughly justified in doing, your dignity being not merely injured, but utterly trampled on—the slave-merchant (a.k.a. "bookseller") will use his whip mercilessly to teach you sense. The customer's hands are slithering all over you, squeezing you and slipping into any place he feels like—no part of you is off-limits: the man wants, presumably, to make sure you are well-fed, healthy, with all your wits about you, unblemished, with a full set of teeth (this point is inspected with especial care, as in the sale of horses, because if the face-powder lies, the teeth don't).

The worst of it is that even after he's had his paws all over you like that, he is, in fact, under no obligation whatsoever to buy you, nor even to explain why you are not to his liking. He simply returns you to the bookseller, then starts checking out some other slave girl, or walks out of the shop. It isn't always choosiness on their part. There's the occasional genuine psychopath among the customers: the minute he steps over the threshold, you can see in his eyes that he hasn't come to buy anyone, only to give rein to his perversion. And if, in addition, he is wearing a longish raincoat, even in midsummer, and he looks sort of sloppy and untidy, with long greasy hair and an unshaven face, there can be no doubt: he's one of them!

Salespeople are also quite aware what kind of person they are dealing with, and would happily throw him out of the bookshop. This isn't out of any consideration for us—what do they care for our humiliation and indignity?—but because they don't like to have their own time wasted. They are serious businessmen, time is money for them, but they can never be entirely sure: any individual is a potential buyer until proven otherwise, and besides, the competition is eagerly waiting for them to slip up one way or another.

Customers of this sort are inclined to spend a whole hour or more in the bookshop. And they generally molest the youngest books, those only very recently arrived, still virtually children. Sometimes, if the bookshop is crowded and the bookseller's attention is distracted, these pedophiles slink into a corner and stay there doing their thing until their urges are completely satisfied. (Recently a few bookshops, wishing to justify their pretensions as "parlors," have taken to providing special booths for this sort of activity.) The freak reads the poor little underage girl through and through, and leaves her destitute, ruined forever; deflowered as she is, no-one will even want to look at her any more, let alone buy her.

*La poveretta* ends up in the warehouse as a shop-soiled, useless copy, waiting to be written off and then dispatched to her final destiny from which there is no reprieve, unless an employee takes her home out of pity, and with no intention of reading her—that would be out of the question, he has his own dignity to protect, even in acts of mercy there are levels below which he will not sink. But it's a free copy, it might serve some purpose or other, perhaps as a birthday present to some other human, especially if she is nicely done up in colorful gift-wrap so that it isn't immediately apparent that she has been used already.

The main adversaries of the slave merchants are, naturally, thieves. Enemies of our enemies are our friends, so it's no wonder if we feel a certain liking for the species. Perhaps we even take things a little too far. Our feelings for them are too romantically tinged, we see them as handsome bandits who rob the rich in order to give to the poor. Among us, they are always called Robin. We could have chosen some other name, human history is replete with robbers, but the verbal similarity seems to have played its part.

It can't be helped: when you are in slavery, you tend to idealize your liberator, particularly if you are a sentimental female, which most of us, unfortunately, are. It turns out, however, that not every Robin is a nice guy. The gentleman among them might be stealing you in order to reserve you for his own, exclusive use and possession, or at least to present you as a gift to someone he loves, but gentlemen are few and far between. The motives of most shoplifters are far from noble: the legendary honor among thieves has in fact little evidence to support it. They are looking to sell you off as soon as possible, to any buyer, for a price so low it is a further insult.

Though admittedly, in this instance we are responsible, and we can't shift the blame onto anyone else. For a start, we are complicit in the kidnapping, because we did have an opportunity to alert the sales assistant at the moment of the theft but simply preferred to keep mum. What slave in her right mind would call out the guards against her own rescuer, whatever destiny awaited her at his hands? Besides, we have been warned from our youth that the love of bandits—just like their honor—is generally unreliable. A hurricane of love it may be, while it lasts; but in most cases it does not last long. Yet what female heart follows the dictates of reason?

Nor are thieves the only ones to reduce our prices. Booksellers do it too, when they notice that the "merchandise" is slow to leave the shelves. Their euphemism for it is "discount." This phenomenon was more or less tolerable in the early days, when it only occurred rarely and for good reasons, such as a book-fair. Market forces, though, had their effect, and the money-men started to compete in thinking up various excuses for price-cuts, given that they would increase sales.

The book-fair price reductions lasted one week initially, then expanded into a fortnight, then a whole month, but even after that the salespeople didn't adhere rigidly to the calendar, so that often the October discounts lasted well into December. As it really wouldn't do to sell books using the same explanation in February too, they had to think up further excuses. And, as it turned out, that was not at all difficult to do.

Public holidays were a good occasion: a Christmas discount was introduced, then the discount for Women's Day, and a "price slash" or a "clearance sale" linked to Labor Day. It wasn't long before a peculiar anomaly became apparent. The most popular books during such low-price periods had very little to do with the nominal occasion. During the Christmas price reductions, for example, people rushed to buy illustrated books about how to raise non-blooming houseplants; also much in demand that season were studies in hermeneutics, especially those referring to poetics.

Puzzled booksellers hardly had any time to get to grips with this, because the 8th March, Women's Day, had already arrived, and people flocked to buy late Renaissance Oriental anthropology, plus computer manuals, particularly if a can of keyboard-cleaning spray could be had free with the book. Looking into the results of May 1st, Labor Day, sales, bookshop owners finally abandoned any attempt to make sense of such unpredictable trends in popular demand. Who indeed could have foreseen that at the beginning of spring, humans would clamor to buy surfboarding handbooks, as well as knitting and embroidery guides, though only those well-illustrated with patterns?

To the horror of book business entrepreneurs, demand was completely out of kilter with supply in all three of these cut-price campaigns. Nobody wanted the cut-price books, while those books that everybody wanted were unavailable at any price. To be sure, it's far from flattering when nobody wants you even at a discount, but for this humiliation we were compensated in part by maliciously observing the torments of the booksellers. When you are in servitude, and waiting humbly and meekly for a buyer to come and claim you, nothing will cheer you up more than the crestfallen look on the salesperson's face while he is explaining to an irate customer that right at this moment he does not have the sort of slave-girl the customer requires.

Despite these disastrous adventures, the book people didn't give up. They hunted for further excuses to cut prices. National holidays were next—and for the first time a certain amount of rational feedback was obtained: the biggest sellers were encyclopedias of strong drink, lexicons of light firearms (and of heavy weapons too) and "Home Doctor" type books, especially those with an extensive chapter on ways to purge an over-loaded stomach.

Church holidays were quickly abandoned as sales-campaign opportunities, because buyers displayed extremely blasphemous tendencies at such times. Nobody wanted to buy books about spiritual disciplines and the afterlife, not to mention ones that concentrated on questions of honor and justice; people avoided them as though the copies were infected with the plague. But precisely at such times buyers asked, mainly in low, conspiratorial and profane tones, for explicit sex manuals, stressing the need for clear photographs—or, at the very least, color illustrations.

In this race for excuses, all restraint was ultimately lost, especially in small, out-of-the-way bookshops with low overheads and correspondingly poor sales. They were willing to stoop to anything. In such establishments, discounts were given to honor Bee-Keepers' Day, Stamp-Collectors' and Numismaticians' Day, International Savings Day, Stonemasons' and Dynamiters' Day, Winegrowers' Day, Anti-Mosquito Action Day, Flautists' Day, House-Pets' Day, Stage Magicians' Day, Glass-Blowers' Day, Human Rights Day, Car Electricians' and Lacquer-Sprayers' Day, Clowns' Day, Bird Migration Day and so forth.

As so often happens in human affairs, once things had absolutely gone too far someone recognized that all the excuses were, in fact, unnecessary, not to mention meaningless, so they declared a week of discounts for no reason at all. Just because. Discounts for the sake of discounts. Business rivals quickly responded by offering ten days, then two weeks, then one month of discounts, a whole season of discounts, a year, five years of discount, a Discount Decade.

Slogans like "Price-Slash till the End of the Century" or even "till the end of the Millennium" sounded very impressive, but these were exaggerations, of course, mere promotional gimmicks: at that time, less than a year and a half was left to the end of both the century and the millennium. As there was no further progress to be made in this direction—talk of eons or kalpas would only have confused the public—the booksellers made the last available offer: they proclaimed a permanent discount, without time-limit. Discount *ad infinitum*.

But discounts are not the most serious form of degradation for the poor slave-girls in the bookshops. There is something worse: THE SALE. This is when we plummet into an abyss of humiliation. As self-respecting individuals, though in captivity, even our original prices are deeply hurtful to us, no matter how high they might be. What, Mister Bookman thinks this is all we are worth? Well, he'll see, what miserably low prices, he could have asked three times as much, we're going to sell like hot cakes.

If this doesn't happen sharpish, we turn our anger on the buyers. So what are they waiting for then, do they expect to get us for nothing maybe? If they don't have the money, why do they keep slaves? These days any idiot wants to be a slave-owner. We'll end up in a fine mess, the way things are headed. Really going to the dogs. The slave-merchants, basically, are filled with the same sort of annoyance, although they express it in different language, and so a strange phenomenon emerges: we become allies, at least for a little while, hardly a very natural relationship.

It would no doubt flatter our vanity the most if we could stay on the bookshop shelves forever, proudly defying the stinginess of the buyers, but unfortunately, the camaraderie between us and the merchants is of short duration. Practical men that they are, they don't let themselves be ruled by their emotions for long, nor do they have much time in which to do so. When they see that the merchandise isn't shifting, they try discounts, and if that fails then there's no other option, a sale there must be.

What an indignity it is! First they adorn the shop-window with lurid announcements consisting largely of spectacularly crossed-out old prices, those very same original prices that we were so miffed about, and then, printed in larger letters, the new prices, so low that we turn our gaze away in shame, refusing to believe that we have been so deeply degraded in a single night. The proverbial come-down from a horse to a mule, or from pillar to post is as nothing compared to this plunge.

As if this weren't enough, they sometimes even install a speaker above the entrance from which to entice passers-by all day long, complete with appropriate music, like the hustlers outside third-rate brothels. They haven't yet taken to tugging at the punters' sleeves, but that will be the next logical step.

Something very similar does happen, in fact: the bookshop manager sends the most junior member of his staff out into the street, armed with a heap of promotional leaflets full of aggressive slogans, printed in italics and sometimes even in verse; the young person is charged with distributing a certain number of leaflets in a certain length of time. In order to achieve this, the novice bookseller does his best to stuff the leaflets almost forcibly into the unwilling hands of passers-by. This mode of promotion is not abandoned even when the pavement over a broad semi-circle in front of the shop becomes thickly covered with a snow of discarded leaflets, many of them crumpled in disgust.

Not that it fails totally. Humans are, in general, great lovers of sales, thanks to their tendency to seize and carry off just about anything if the price is sufficiently lowered, even things for which they have absolutely no need or desire—especially those things, in fact. Come the sales, bookshops fill up with all sorts of eager beavers, some of whom rarely or never visit a bookshop at any other time. The place heaves, booksellers rub their palms in satisfaction, and we have to endure all sorts of new unpleasantness. But what can you do? In every battle someone is the loser.

Amongst the new clientele there are a few fellows with somewhat peculiar requests. They are choosy, but not like regular punters. They remain on the whole indifferent to the titles or even the contents of the volumes offered in the shop. They care not at all for such trifles as authors, co-authors, translators, publishers, editors, anthologists, preface or afterword writers—least of all for proofreaders and copy-editors.

The thing these customers enquire about—after the price—is style and color. Of binding, of course. Leather is much in demand, although canvas does not lag very far behind; the horse chestnut sort of glossy brown color is a favorite, because it complements almost all kinds of wood. And if the title is embossed on the cover in gold leaf (or an imitation thereof) it is as if you have implanted a gold tooth in their gob free of charge. One particular requirement is that there should be a long series of volumes in identical format: such customers love multi-tome editions. This is why they have introduced a new system of measurement: by the meter rather than by the unit. The metric system is relentlessly encroaching into every area of life.

A buyer walks in with a precise measurement, as if entering a drapist's, and the seller extracts a tool from a remote corner of the bottom drawer, one that he keeps especially for such occasions: a spool of extendable metallic tape, calibrated in centimeters. Sometimes there are problems with the measurements, books are not rolls of cloth and cannot be tailored like cloth to the nearest millimeter; but if the buyer isn't keen to have all the volumes in a set, which he almost never is, and if the seller is skillful and experienced, the business can, in the end, be completed almost to perfection: the customer gets 1.27 meters of books, which will somehow fit into a 1.25 meter shelf in his living-room, inside the biggest item of furniture, something like a massive cabinet or dresser, shiny, very tall, and described in some parts of the world as "regal." The most important dimension is the height: that can't be squeezed.

Though we should, seemingly, be deeply hurt by this method of sale—one of its downsides is that it tends to separate and break up some of our happy extended families—it does have its advantages. In fact, to be owned by humans who have bought you by the meter is the equivalent of a major win on the lottery, as compared with other fates that may befall us during a sale. These metric owners are, give or take, the best that we can hope for.

For a start, longevity is guaranteed with them, because nobody will ever open, let alone read us. In homes like these we serve a purely ornamental purpose. Like a ship in a bottle, for instance, or a stuffed boar's head. They put us on the shelves, possibly behind glass. (The space available may be a little tight, but you always have to put up with something.) Then they show us off proudly to their friends and relatives: how nicely we fit into the ambience. And they are even more chuffed because of the price they paid for us.

Our cleanliness, there on the shelf, is carefully seen to, not a great hardship because there are only a few of us. We receive thorough and regular dustings, along with all the rest of the furniture, not like those huge libraries that some intellectual bookworms cram wall-to-wall and floor-to-ceiling into their rooms, where a duster enters maybe once in three years and then only cursorily; and when someone pulls out one of the less-frequented tomes, he gets an instant asthma attack.

There is a special kind of bookshop where everything is on permanent sale: the antiquarian ones. They're dreary, gloomy places, true geriatric homes for books. The slaves arriving for sale in such places are nearly all in a very sad condition: aged, decrepit, used up, moldy, often with serious physical defects. If only her covers are gone, or a page or two, she's in relatively good shape; but there are seriously crippled books, with the entire preface and afterword missing, and some have even lost entire chapters. Who would pay that much for them, then? It isn't even a case of selling, it's more like "make me an offer."

But the selling price is still a blessing compared to the buying price. Comes a citizen, a simple soul, and offers to sell his personal library, one that he has been collecting for many years; hard times have forced him to this desperate measure. Then he hears what the antiquarian is prepared to offer for his collection—a well-preserved one, much loved, gently tended, imbued with touching associations—and he stands there gaping, astounded, shattered, stupefied. He simply cannot believe his ears. And, of course, initially he refuses, he won't even consider it, turns on his heel and stalks out in defiance. Sometimes he even slams the door behind him.

The antiquarian responds with an indifferent shrug; he's an old hand, he's long ago become inured to such outbursts. He knows the citizen will return. And indeed the citizen does return, generally speaking the very next day, as soon as his ruffled feathers have smoothed down a bit. He's really under the cosh, his problems are multiplying and there's no ready cash, the family must survive somehow, the children must go on the school trip, the pantry must be stocked with food for the winter, the car exhaust is shot, and the wife expects to go skiing, she can't stand the frustration of a winter without it. Though the offer is pure robbery, highway robbery, there is no other option.

A touching farewell scene ensues. We are not much moved by human suffering—why should we be, given the way they treat us?—yet our hearts are not of stone. We can't hold back the tears as we watch him promise his protégées, in a voice all shaky and trembling, that this parting is only temporary, he will buy them back very soon, as soon as circumstances improve, he won't let them stay in here forever, they will all be together again one day.

And indeed, the first few days he comes to the antiquarian bookshop regularly to visit his books; he knows exactly where they have been placed; he fondles them a little, smooths them, blows the dust away, even whispers a few endearments when nobody is watching, and when one day he sees that one is missing, that she has been sold, a sob escapes him, a whimper from the bottom of his soul, as if he has lost one of his nearest and dearest. A truly poignant sight, which sends a shiver through us.

But nothing lasts forever with humans; not even pain. First his visits become fewer, less regular, and then, for a long time, he does not come at all. He vanishes, as if the ground has swallowed him up. When he does finally appear, he is a quite different man. He pretends not to recognize anyone, as if the entire drama had never taken place; he browses leisurely through the books, perhaps even buys one. But never one of those he sold at such a shamefully low price.

It might seem that we books loathe and fear these antiquarians as the nadir of our fortunes. Indeed, we are never held so cheap as in these dim, untidy, gloomy chambers where only the incense is lacking in order to complete the atmosphere of a chapel of rest. And such would truly be the case, were it not for the bizarre human compulsion to collect ancient rarities.

Quite out of the blue, in precisely the place where we lose all caste, where all hope deserts us, a transformation occurs; not all that often, but still, a transformation worthy of a fairytale. Like Cinderella, perhaps, but with a few discrepancies. No slipper, for a start, and what's more there may be several princes vying feverishly for just one of us. This fortunate sister is most favored if she is the last of her kind, and if in addition she is very old, two and a half centuries at least. There's a real market for that sort of age-group.

The buyers aren't really interested in her text or in her soul; they don't even care much for her outward appearance. She doesn't have to be beautiful, although it's desirable to be reasonably well-preserved. They just wish to own her, they and nobody else, to make sure nobody else lays hold of her. And they are prepared to pay any price. To a passionate collector the question of price is beneath them.

The pursuit of such rare books is, in fact, the true métier of antiquarians. All the rest is a sideshow, a facade almost. The really big profits are made when the original owner has no inkling as to the real value of the book. Some ignorant, naive person—the widow of a university professor, for instance, a woman whose old age pension is, if not small, then a bit on the scanty side. She has decided to sell the entire library of her deceased husband. This with the intention of improving her financial situation somewhat.

She is well aware that by doing so she is violating a solemn oath. Upon his death-bed the husband extracted from her a binding vow that she would never sell the books; the two of them having no heir, she should bequeath the library to a museum or some similar institution, preferably one of national importance; or she should even establish a foundation dedicated to preserving the professor's legacy. But her conscience doesn't bother her unduly, even though he's probably tossing and turning in his grave right now; it serves him right, he spent his entire life devoting far more attention to those damned piles of printed paper than he ever did to her. She certainly has no intention of reading them, so why should they merely collect dust? This way at least she will get some benefit from them, it's time she got a life at last, after wasting all her best years pandering to him.

The antiquarian pays the widow a call, as is only fitting; she surely won't lug all these tomes over to his shop, and how could she, anyway? It is incumbent upon him to bring a bunch of flowers, preferably narcissi—no elderly lady anywhere fails to delight in narcissi—and perhaps a nicely-wrapped *bonbonniere* as well, tied with colored ribbon frilled above the knot, if he expects a particularly good deal. You must speculate to accumulate. Only fools expect to succeed without investment.

The conversation absolutely must not start with business. Business comes last. Skillfully, the antiquarian first gets the old lady to tell him the entire story of her life. She is very eager to do so, of course, since so few people visit her, she talks mainly to her cats. They are no proper audience for her woes. So there she sits, pouring her heart out, undismayed that it is to a stranger; the gentleman is so nice to her, so full of understanding, so open. When was the last time, indeed, that a man brought her flowers? Not to mention the *bonbonniere*, although the doctor has strictly forbidden her any sweets because of her high blood-sugar, but never mind, it won't go to waste.

He listens attentively, sincerely sympathizes with her sorrows, is appalled at how badly she was treated by her inconsiderate husband. He concurs with all her opinions and completely agrees that people in general have sunk into wickedness and greed. They only want to cheat you, however they can—you can't trust anyone any more, the world has become totally corrupt.

When, at least three hours and fifteen minutes after his arrival, the library finally comes up for discussion, the lady is almost ready to give it to him for nothing. Moreover, she is truly grateful to him for helping her get rid of this enormous quantity of books. He stands up to take a look at the books, performing this duty in a seemingly casual manner. He skims lightly, almost incuriously over them; but in fact he is keenly scanning for rarities. If he does spot one, he reacts no more noticeably than a top professional poker-player.

Having completed the inspection, he doesn't immediately declare his offer. First the details of transportation must be gone into. That's a much more important question than the price. The lady should leave all the practicalities to his men; they are experienced, they know their work, of course they will bring cardboard boxes and a truck, they will even bring along a vacuum cleaner so that not a speck of dust will remain on the shelves after they have gone, and if madam wishes, they can even carry away the shelves so they will not remain conspicuously empty; of course they will be perfectly quiet, the neighbors will not even notice that the books are being carried out.

When the antiquarian, finally, proclaims the price, the old lady will not even hear it. She will just nod briefly to indicate her agreement, but her eyes will be lowered, because she will feel embarrassed that these concluding trivialities have to take place at all. He will then gallantly pull out his banknotes, all crisp and of large denomination, and place them upon the table. She will pick them up only long after his departure, and stash them in a small wooden box ornately and deeply carved, and locked with a very small key, in which she keeps her cash. Actually to count out the banknotes would be unthinkable. How would that look? As he takes his leave he will, according to etiquette, kiss her hand.

Many would accuse this antiquarian of cheating her, but we don't subscribe in the least to such po-faced moralizing. Quite the reverse, he's a genuine benefactor so far as we're concerned, and if he profits a little in the course of helping others, why should anyone begrudge him it? Besides, we ask you, what has he actually done wrong? Did he steal anything? No. Did he force the old woman to accept his offer? No. He just failed to inform her that one or two books in her library were exceedingly valuable. Was he under any obligation to do so, though? We can't blame him for demonstrating exactly the same qualities that, in other businessmen, we praise as skill, shrewdness, nous.

Anyway, what would the old lady do with the large sum of money she might have obtained had she known what she had in her possession? She couldn't spend it in her lifetime, and she couldn't take it with her to the grave. For her, the money would merely be a burden, she would live in fear that someone might rob her of it, or that inflation might render it worthless, or that she might get begging letters from distant cousins she hasn't laid eyes on in years, and whose faces she can't even remember—any more than she can recall precisely how they are related to her.

As it is, she has received enough cash to repair her washing machine, which for years now has only functioned on one cycle, and even that is getting unreliable. She will also buy a decent overcoat, perhaps even one with a fur collar, and she may replace the worn out linoleum in the kitchen that she is always tripping over because the edges are curled up. If, on top of all this, she can find a good package holiday for two weeks in a spa, out of season, that would be splendid, her rheumatism has been playing her up lately.

Add to this the balmy spiritual effect of the pleasant conversation with the nice gentleman, and the old woman has every reason to be satisfied. As, in fact, has

Cinderella, who will, thanks to the antiquarian's expertise, henceforth be treated as she deserves, as a princess, rather than languishing in the dead professor's study where, after his wife's demise, she might have fallen into the hands of barbarians who wouldn't even recognize her blue blood. Or she might even have been dumped in a rubbish skip.

No, she will swiftly be separated from the other books, she will never find herself consorting with them on common shelves or tables in the bookshop, among cheap goods intended for common buyers. She will be whisked away to safety, into a steel safe of the type money is kept in; and that very same day a restoration expert will come to examine her. Under tight security he will clean and fix her up, so that she gives the best possible impression of being well-preserved.

His preparations complete, the antiquarian will phone his selected clientele. He never comes out and gives them the news point-blank, he uses special code words settled on by prior agreement: this is a top secret affair, and you never know who might be eavesdropping on the telephone line. The conversation is brief and to the point, identical with each of the five men.

"I have obtained a bottle of excellent French wine from the year 1762. Would you like to drop by tonight and taste it?"

From the other end of the line, first a few moments of dead silence, then a little cough rather resembling a death-rattle, then a hoarse question: "At seven to nine, as usual?"

The antiquarian chuckles inaudibly to himself, and answers curtly: "As usual." He never ever rubs his palms together. He is a man of refinement, even when nobody is watching.

The antiquarian bookshop lies inconspicuously down a small alley, and at eight o'clock, moreover, it closes and remains locked and unlit all night. And yet, at precisely seven minutes to nine, five silhouettes, with raincoat collars up and hat-brims down, assemble at its door, each arriving from a different direction. No greetings are exchanged. No-one speaks a word.

A hand rises and gives a muffled knock, three short ones and two long, then one more short. Just to heighten the suspense, nothing happens for several long moments, then the door opens with a barely audible creak, and the visitors slip through it, silent as shadows. The last of them safe inside, a head pokes out, reconnoiters left and right, and quickly withdraws. Within, no lights are lit. For a brief second a shaft beams from the antiquarian's back office as the guests enter.

The protocol is well practiced, and refined down to the smallest detail. Five comfortable armchairs are arranged in a semicircle. Beside each is a small table, and on it a bottle of mineral water, a bottle-opener, a glass, inverted and placed on a paper napkin, and a folder containing several photographs. Before the chairs stands a painter's easel draped in black velvet. A strong spotlight is directed at the easel. There is no other source of light. The visitors seat themselves in silence, everyone knows which chair is intended for whom, there are no unnecessary movements.

The antiquarian stands patiently by the easel while the guests consult the photos of the first page of text and of the title page. Two of them use eye-glasses, one adopts a monocle. They contemplate the pictures deeply, turn them this way and that, bring them closer and then hold them farther away. One pulls out a magnifying glass in which the spotlight's beam sparkles and flashes for an instant. Finally, they all return the pictures to the folders.

The antiquarian takes two deep breaths before lifting the black cover. Suddenly magnetized, five shapes lean forward in the dusk as one. For some time they remain frozen, as though posing for a Caravaggio. Finally the host clears his throat a little, and the auction starts.

The only sound to be heard is his voice. Everything else is facial expressions, inconspicuous gestures: an eyebrow is raised, a fingertip taps a nose, a foot is repositioned across the other foot. Expertly the host translates these signals into numbers, and the numbers rise, slowly at first, then faster, then dizzyingly fast. At last, a mere two and a half minutes later, there is no further movement, no more signs. All is still and silent once again. The antiquarian waits a few more seconds, he gazes keenly at the semicircle of chairs, then once more clears his throat, quite quietly. In the ears of the guests it is the bang of a gavel.

The host approaches one of them and, with a slight bow, extends his hand to shake. Then the rest congratulate the winner; still no words are spoken. All remove their gloves before the handshake, and all bow just as slightly; one clicks the heels of his tall boots. Their hats, however, remain upon their heads. Then they leave the office in single file, pass through the main part of the bookshop, and out into the street. They glance around, turn up their raincoat collars a little higher, pull their hat-brims down a little lower, and swiftly depart in five different directions, without either benediction or valediction. On the tables the bottles of mineral water remain perfectly untouched. As always.

The formalities are completed the next day. Employees see to that. At eleven fifteen a uniformed courier arrives. He moves through the shop with long, almost military strides, looking neither left nor right. He enters the office, but says nothing. He has no need to. Everything is known. He hands the antiquarian an envelope containing a check. Nothing is written on the envelope, which is plain white, glued shut, and identified only by a small embossed coat of arms in the upper left-hand corner.

The antiquarian hands him a package in return, also unmarked, but fastened with a cord. Everything is very quickly concluded. Neither looks to see what is inside, of course; this is between gentlemen. The antiquarian merely nods his unsmiling head. The courier's face remains expressionless. He turns on his heel and strides out. In front of the shop a car waits with its engine running. He drives off fast.

When Cinderella is brought to the Prince's house, she finds herself in a land of milk and honey. She will get her own glass case with its own controlled atmospheric environment. The air moisture is monitored in particular, since moisture and dust are the two greatest enemies of books. A restorer visits her regularly, gives her a thorough examination and applies the necessary prophylactic measures. He uses surgical gloves, tweezers, camel-hair brushes, pleasantly-scented powders. He alone is authorized to touch her.

No-one will get to read her ever again. Of course not. She is sometimes put on display, though only briefly, at special viewings for a select audience of cognoscenti. Only they are capable of appreciating her exquisite qualities. On these occasions everyone wears gauze surgical masks and special slippers. She feels like a rare animal from an endangered species, kept in an elite cage at the zoo.

This heavenly idyll, of course, is the ultimate human hypocrisy. Animals in a zoo have all they need, it's true—who cares about freedom, if three meals a day are guaranteed and you don't have to do any work?—but do the gentlemen in question really believe that the pampering of a single rhinoceros or one lonely giraffe can erase from the record the murder of thousands of their unfortunate fellows in the wilderness? What is the royal treatment accorded one book in comparison with, let's say, the mass extermination that our poor cousins, the schoolbooks, undergo each year?

The schoolbooks' evil destiny is not evident from their birth. Quite the contrary. To the uninitiated eye it might even seem that they look forward to a bright future. A sale is quite a marginal phenomenon compared to the unbelievable rush, lasting several days, of thousands of humans to buy up schoolbooks when each autumn starts. This is especially hectic in those countries where people leave everything to the last possible moment, and such countries are hardly few in number. Classes are just about to commence, but only now are schoolbooks appearing in the bookshops. And never all of them. At least a third are invariably delayed. The quantities that do turn up are just sufficient to drive the pupils, not to mention their eager parents, crazy.

At first light, an extraordinary queue of sudden book-lovers masses in front of the bookshop. As opening time approaches, order breaks down; pushing, shoving and elbowing increase, whipped up by pungent verbal exchanges. The moment the panicked manager finally works up the courage to open the door just a little, a surge of humanity forces him to take shelter as fast as he can behind his rampart, the broad, heavy counter. Within the hugely overcrowded shop the melee degenerates immediately into chaos.

Flying through the air are various items of clothing and other small, unsecured possessions regarded as essential for long waits: caps, shoes, coins, lighters, medals, umbrellas, spectacles, keys, rattles, wigs, nail-clippers, hip-flasks, stools, wedding rings, tobacco pipes, gaiters, newspapers, brooches, season tickets and bus passes, thermos flasks, chamber-pots, key rings, handkerchiefs, badges, drop ear-rings, thermometers, snuff-boxes, dummies, corkscrews, false teeth, cigarette-cases, pocket-knives, hairpins, curtain rings, business cards, hot water bottles and an unknown number of torn-off buttons.

The screeching and yapping can be heard three

streets away, and there's an inevitable outbreak of pinching, tripping, biting, scuffling, wrestling (mostly in an attempt to strangle) and even fistfights, which may occasionally become serious. But no weapons are drawn, whether cold steel or guns; those gathered here are peaceful people, family men. In any case, there are children present, for whom such a spectacle would be unedifying.

The police don't intervene in this academic debate: education, and culture in general, lie outside their remit. A patrol hovers at the edge of the crowd, very dignified, quietly eating their breakfast, which consists mainly of sausage rolls and yoghurt. The policemen are patiently awaiting the first definite indication of a public disturbance: the shattering of one of the large plate-glass window panes. Only then do they start swinging their truncheons.

It isn't easy for a school textbook to retain her presence of mind in the face of such overwhelming popularity—as if she were a film or pop star, or a soccer star at least. She never even makes it to the shelves: the brown paper packaging in which the books were delivered is torn open and then, still warm from the printing-press, she and the rest are thrust into the feverishly extended hands, into the clasp of incandescent admirers. She is completely intoxicated, dizzy, in a trance. The whole world revolves around her.

But, as has been amply demonstrated (though few recognize the fact until it's too late), all fame has its price, and the downfall is directly proportionate to the rise. This glamorous and turbulent initiation over, the rest of the schoolbook's brief, miserable existence is an unqualified disaster.

For a book, there is no fate worse than to be placed in the hands of a schoolchild. Sentimentally prejudiced in favor of their offspring, humans are apt to say, when forced to criticize their young, that children are immature. Immature, indeed! That would be a fulsome compliment! They are veritable vandals, savages—they are monsters! Why doesn't anyone ask us? We know best what schoolchildren are like, year after year we receive first-hand experience of their immaturity.

There is no evil that these little sadists will not perform on a poor textbook in the scant two semesters that they spend together. The whole gamut of book-mauling and book-torture is employed in its most concentrated form: underlining, doodling, twisting and rolling up, folding over, crumpling, tearing off, ripping apart. Frustrated that they cannot vent their anger directly on their teachers, who force them to do the most loathsome work in the world, learning, the children attack us instead. Which is much better than suppressing their rage and becoming traumatized adults.

What takes place at the end of the school year, though, is nothing less than mass slaughter. As soon as the last buzzer *drrrings*, roving bands of pupils start dismembering the poor books in a frenzy of tearing and slashing; then they arrogantly throw their bodies around, until the ground turns white with the strewn insides of gutted books. And adult humans observe the entire carnage benevolently, even with a touch of approval: school's out, the youngsters are releasing their pent-up emotions.

If it so happens that a schoolbook survives these atrocities, she soon comes to regret it. She comes to envy her sisters who died quickly. Because before long she finds herself on the pavement where used schoolbooks are sold for next to nothing, which is inevitably followed by one more year of hell. This is avoided only in those sophisticated societies where educational reforms follow on each other's heels unceasingly, requiring new, updated schoolbooks to be produced each year, the truth contained in the old schoolbooks becoming, thankfully, null and void.

There are some places which possess not a single bookshop, though other bastions of learning and literacy do exist in these human communities. There are cinemas, inns, churches, petrol stations, libraries, barber's shops, galleries and groceries. Sometimes there is even a small theatre, with no balcony or boxes, and, for a long time since, no performances—not even of the meager repertoire it used to offer—but by some inexplicable miracle, bookshops are not to be found. Riding to the rescue comes a special breed of men: travelling slavers—the book salesmen.

Life in captivity is never joyous, of course, but with the slavers it is at least not monotonous. For a start, we get to travel a lot, we are constantly on the move, which is a privilege unavailable to most books. Most of our compatriots spend their whole lives enclosed within four walls, never once even poking their noses outside, as if they were agoraphobic. Their situation is worse than that of a housewife who at least gets to visit the fruit and vegetable market from time to time, if nothing else.

We, on the other hand, are constantly on the road, where there is never a dearth of entertainment. It's really hard, at times, to maintain the serious demeanor which is quite properly expected of us, while we observe our master stretching his eloquence in an effort to dump us on someone—anyone at all. He and his like would be the last men in the world actually to read a book, as no-one knows better than we. They even have their justification—the motto of their guild, almost—though for obvious reasons, they never voice it in public: "Isn't it enough that I have to sell them, I really can't be expected to read them, too!" But if you heard how they recommend or praise one of us to a possible buyer, you'd think they were well-read, not to mention true experts, particularly in psychology.

One of the most important things, so far as they

are concerned, is that our covers should scream with color, while our titles should be as vague and uninformative as possible. That way, we can be made to meet the needs of every customer. Outstanding recent favorites included *The Meaning of Existence* (an essay in post-modern philosophy) and *In the Future We Trust* (a theological tract about life beyond the grave). The former had on its cover, quite appropriately, a photograph of a sunset on a lush tropical island full of palm trees, and the latter a well-fed family group, smiling broadly, arms draped across each other's shoulders, gazing vaguely into a starry sky. To think how *many* of these two books sold, mainly to all sorts of delighted women readers!

As a matter of fact, this kind of transaction isn't exactly hard work for the salesman. Everything hangs on the gullibility of the ignorant victims. When secretaries from some ill-lit municipal office, or waitresses from some fly-infested bistro on the bus station, look at the books on offer, they only take account of the outward appearance, never bothering to leaf through them, and their first question is always the same: Has the book any romance, any love interest?

Even were the salesman to experience qualms of conscience over the deception he is intending (he never does, of course), sensitive fellow that he is, he just wouldn't have the heart to disappoint them. Their eyes smolder like coals in their longing to hear him say "Yes." So who is he to deny them?

And when they hear, what's more, that the books can be paid for monthly by installments, and that they, the buyers, need only make a modest down payment and sign a contract in order to have the book given to them on the spot, the transaction is completed without delay. The bookseller then stows the papers and cash in his attaché case and makes off with the hurried stride of a businessman with no time to waste. He leaves us in the lurch, of course, but that's even less of a burden on his mind.

First we have to endure the outrage of disappointed readers, who masochistically persevere well into the third page of densely packed mental torture (no more than five paragraphs within those three pages) before the realization dawns on them that there will be no love story in the book, despite the salesman's heartfelt assurance and the inviting cover. Then they take their anger out on us, even though we are the least guilty of all the parties; punishments vary, the least being banishment to some far-flung corner, where we are entirely forgotten, like an embarrassing faux pas.

Then there are the subsequent payments, an even more sordid affair. Some of the women, duped as they have been, resolutely draw the line at these and refuse to make the installments, which means that ultimately the whole thing ends up in court; where even we, the books, are bound over to be summoned, sometimes even as the accused party, which is hardly a very pleasant experience. What self-respecting book would want to be dragged through the courts, even as a witness?

Although basically humiliating, bookshops are not the worst places where books are bought and sold. With all the unpleasantness we are liable to go through there, at least we can count on having a roof over our heads, no small thing when you compare it with an outdoor market, which might be held in all sorts of places.

A prolonged period in the open air can be disastrous for the health of a book, even if the weather is fine and dry, let alone wet and windy, rainy or snowy. Then we catch all sorts of illnesses. Coughs and sneezes are unpleasant enough, if relatively harmless; but when we spend day after day under a clear or cloudy sky we come down with much worse things: 'flu, pneumonia, even tuberculosis.

Of course, this never moves the hearts of most of the cold-blooded street-traders who force us, naked as we are, without a shred of clothing, freezing and with our teeth chattering, to lure the buyers, until the actual rain begins—or snow. Only then will his majesty condescend to pull some nylon sheeting over us, not out of any concern for our well-being, but in order to protect his own interests. If we are totally ruined, if we succumb to some deadly disease, no-one will want us any more, we will become worthless, and that for him will be a net loss.

There are other dangers when you find yourself on the street. About the best thing that can happen is that you'll fall into the hands of that breed of merchant known as "collectors." That they are, basically, traders, cannot be denied, but at least they have a certain feeling for books, and occasionally they show a surprising degree of responsibility. Besides, their stalls are not completely open, or totally isolated, but partially covered and grouped together, so we are tucked up safely out of the weather. Sometimes there is even heating.

In addition to this the collectors tend to choose attractive locations. Often it will be some pretty riverside quay, under a row of linden trees, so if nothing else, a pleasant scent will occasionally waft in; and the view of the river is soothing. Also, as there are no sellers of anything else in the vicinity, just the collectors, the people who drop by actually know what to expect. They will mostly be book-lovers, plus the occasional tourist; but he too behaves himself, he can see right away that this isn't some flea market he's entering.

There's another sort of chap, though, who blunders into the street book-trade without having the first idea about it. These are of another stripe entirely. They may have the best of intentions, but what good are those when they are completely lacking in expertise? It all goes to pot. Some of them, for instance, were only yes-

terday selling hardware. Then, when the market failed
and their profits faltered, they heard that booksellers
were supposed to walk through streets of gold. So they
lurched abruptly into this other trade. They don't know
much about books but, they reckon, it can't be all that
different: selling is selling, merchandise is merchandise, what is there to get worked up about? You buy
cheap and you sell dear—books and nails alike.

They open a stall on the busiest street they can find,
such as a boulevard with plenty of pedestrians and lots
of other stalls nearby; the one to the left sells cosmetics, the one to the right sells paints and lacquers. Then,
on the recommendation of a wholesale dealer, they get
hold of a huge mass of books at a big discount, and
proceed to arrange them into categories, knowing that
customers like to see goods sorted by size and kind.
First heap, big hardcover books; second heap, small
paperbacks; third, illustrated books; fourth, books
that used to have dust-jackets but have lost them; fifth,
coverless books; sixth, stray covers without any pages
inside, and so on. All neat and orderly. A notice above
the stall announces proudly: "Spare parts available!"

So he opens his stall; a nice day, a veritable swarm of
people all around, shampoos to the left and turpentine
to the right fly off the shelves as though they were going
for free—his two neighboring colleagues are working
flat out. Only the books seem to get missed, nobody
stops to look at them. The passers-by, many with bags
in their hands, just take a quick glance and then recoil,
as if from something infected with the plague. They
turn away their heads and quicken their step. In front
of the bookstall a lagoon of empty space opens up, as if
a quarantine flag had been hoisted.

The owner looks this way and that in puzzlement,
he doesn't understand. Everyone has represented this
business to him in glowing terms, sales ought to be
large, profits guaranteed, no risk. People adore books,

the wholesaler told him, people are simply crazy about books, they read whatever they can lay hands on. So what's going on? Finally, an idle stroller stops. He looks at the heaped tomes, not with any particular interest, yet he inquires after one particular title.

The trader stares at him as though he has demanded a metal bolt or a screw with a particular Christian and family name. The trader is aware that books have titles, but it never crossed his mind for an instant that the titles were in the least important. No-one told him. He starts picking through the heaps—what else can he do? Who could possibly memorize all the damned titles in this clutter? He soon becomes agitated, the desired title is nowhere to be seen, and the customer is losing patience too and might leave. "Perhaps another one might do?" the trader asks in desperation. "Here, this one, look how thick it is! And it has pictures! And it isn't very expensive, either."

Yet even this is not the darkest destiny lying in wait for us out on the street. Being sold in any kind of stall is still marginally decent, so we manage to endure the low-life neighbors, the ignoramus of a trader and the crowd shying away from us, although it's still deeply humiliating. What, though, of our poor sisters who are laid out on the bonnet of a car? That's true degradation.

Most of their time is spent inside a vehicle, being transported from one parking-lot to another. The seller keeps them mainly in the boot or on the back seat, where in winter they freeze and in summer they suffocate with the heat. And if the door or the bonnet doesn't shut tightly, and moisture seeps in, we're certain to come down with chronic rheumatism. The bouncing and shaking around, the stink of exhaust fumes, are small hardships by comparison.

The whole day long these books—as many of them as possible—are set out on a blanket over the bonnet, in some city street, out in the open or under a tree.

In fine weather it might look like a bank holiday picnic, if it weren't for the ever-present fear of the police and trading standards officers. The hawker shifts his gaze perpetually back and forth in the hope of spotting the danger just in time. What else can the fellow do? He's operating without a license, moonlighting—there would be no profit if he went legal: taxes are high and income meager.

Over the years he has honed his ability to get wind of them at a great distance, even when they're disguised.

Then he's out of there like lightning, even at the expense of a customer who may be just reaching for his wallet. Without a by your leave the hawker snatches the book from said customer's hands, grabs the four corners of the blanket and with one mighty tug scoops us all up, as if into a sack. He chucks his haul onto the front passenger seat and takes off. Just like that: tires screech, frightened pedestrians scatter in every direction, curses fly from all the other drivers.

We're tumbled and tossed and bruised inside the blanket; we sustain the occasional sprain or concussion, but nobody cares about these minor inconveniences, saving their lives is more important. Anything is better than getting caught; we all know what that means. Who wants to fall into the clutches of the police?

It does happen, though, from time to time. Say, after a few beers on a hot day, the hawker relaxes his guard; nobody's perfect. Then they nab us. Next they confiscate us—as a cautionary example. The hawker doesn't put up too much of a fuss, and it wouldn't do him much good if he did. It could have gone worse for him, he could have ended up in prison—or even worse, they might have impounded his car. He'll get some more books, he'll find the money somehow, and the very next day he'll be back in business; a new car, though, he couldn't even dream of buying.

So he gets away, but we, who have done nothing

wrong, remain at the police station. First they open a file on us: our personal data, fingerprints, photographs (front and profile), and so on. Throughout, they treat us with conspicuous roughness: we get slapped around, punched maybe, a few of the sisters are thoroughly beaten up. For some reason the cops are very brutal with us; they don't like us at all, although we never do anything to deserve it. Actually we try to keep out of their way, since we don't like them either and don't have much in common with them.

Of course, we never get to see an investigating judge and a lawyer is something we can only dream of. Our arrival once documented, the cops sling us straight into a cell where we remain for an indefinite length of time. If we cherish the hope that our incarceration will be brief, that hope is soon dashed when we encounter the other sisters who have been languishing there for many years, with no prospect of liberation or even a fair trial. Abandoned and forgotten by all, they rot slowly in the dank cellar.

They see the light of day only on those rare occasions when the police put them up at a sale of impounded goods. Sales like these are organized every year on Police Day, as a special treat for the most slavishly zealous clerks in the police bureaucracy and for their families. Our prices are extra low, just high enough to be distinguishable from a free perk. Humans come and grab everything and cart it off, things they need and want and things they don't need or want but which are so glamorously cheap they can't resist them. Only the books remain unsold and are returned, every last one of them, to the putrid cellar. No-one even takes a look at them, let alone buys them.

Once upon a time an enlightened, high-ranking policeman, envisioning a modernized force of educated, well-read cops, tried to put a stop to the unedifying revulsion felt by this distinguished profession towards books. Firmly believing that he had plumbed the depths of the police force's corporate soul, this man cunningly ordained that, for every book sold, the buyer should receive a bonus: a toaster, chisel, iron, teapot, corset, trowel, candlestick, hotplate, garden shears, silk lampshade, dog-muzzle, grandfather clock, jump-lead, pepper grinder, hair-clippers, first-aid pack, casserole, tire-iron, or something equally handy.

And, indeed, the books sold out rapidly that day and would have done so even if there had been twice as many; but the policeman himself did not get the promotion he was hoping for. The indefatigable Police Standards Commission discovered all the books (but none of the bonus items) in a skip not far from the police station exit. The fiasco was hushed up; the police force doesn't like washing its dirty laundry in public, and as for the books, they were returned to the cellar under cover of darkness. Because the incident involved such a large number of persons, there was no reprimand.

Yet even car-boot sales, and the possible life imprisonment resulting therefrom, are not the grimmest disgrace which may lie in wait for a book. If you are a decent, self-respecting soul (and books are on the whole) and if you take pride in such virtues as honesty, humility, morality, honor, reputation and faith which ought to characterize every book, then, sad to relate, there is a fate far worse than death: the raincoat sale. This is the nadir. We can go no lower.

Actually, the thing is so horrendous that no book will talk about it, even under duress. You can't make us talk about it. You can try and bribe us as much as you like, you can torture us cruelly, but you'll never succeed in getting a word out of us. However, since it's high time this loathsome matter was aired in public, a voice will be loaned for the purpose. It will be loaned briefly, reluctantly, and it will be a voice entirely unconstrained by revulsion; horrified at nothing; able to stomach anything; tougher than an old infantry boot; utterly insensitive. In short, a human voice.

*(The reading of the next twenty-six paragraphs is strongly disapproved for minors or for persons of a prudish disposition. Owing to the nature of the medium, however, no means are available to prevent their doing so. This is not a movie theatre to which such persons could be denied entry, by force if necessary. If the above mentioned individuals choose to succumb to their rampant curiosity and ignore this warning, we disclaim all responsibility for any unpleasant consequences which may ensue.)*

A lady is walking along in a park somewhere, in broad daylight, preferably a sunny day though that's not essential. This trick always works best in fine weather. The season is early autumn because that, as we know, is the pleasantest time of year, providing a suitable emollient for the gross event which is about to occur. The lady is wearing a wide-brimmed pink hat, very chic, with a large ribbon tied in a bow to one side and a black lace veil half-covering her face.

She is leading a doggie on an extendable leash; possibly a poodle, but any other very small dog will do. The doggie has to be small to fit harmoniously into the general scene. The doggie is wearing a little multi-colored coat, knitted from natural wool, probably a bit too warm for him, but one can't be sure because this doggie doesn't have his tongue lolling out as any common mutt would. This animal is well-groomed, his hair and claws have been manicured, perhaps even powdered.

All is peaceful and calm, no unpleasantness is to be seen, apart from the shortish, balding type approaching her. His face is flushed, a bit puffy, and his wire-rimmed spectacles have small round lenses. He wears a thick toothbrush mustache.

He looks like a post-office clerk, one with a disability

pension perhaps, on account of intractable water on the knee; or a sometime poet who, his high hopes dashed, has turned to drink as the only possible remedy for his chronic lack of inspiration. The man is inconspicuously dressed in a long grey raincoat. That it should be old and torn at the seams is optional, but it must be double-breasted, with two rows of buttons. His hands are thrust deep inside his pockets. There is no hint as to how events will unfold.

Once he is within a few paces of the lady, the man suddenly stops and, in a single vigorous movement, spreads his raincoat wide to left and right. Now he resembles a bat swooping from the top of a nearby horse chestnut tree, only of course much larger. Mademoiselle emits a squeal of alarm, as required by the circumstances, and the doggie first starts back in fright, as if encountering a very angry cat, then runs off behind his mistress's feet (looping the leash around her ankles), from which vantage point he commences growling courageously. A lark, flapping its noisy wings, shoots out from the green hedge surrounding the park. (Well, maybe not a lark, exactly—it flies off too quickly for its identity to be established.)

Contrary to popular expectation, no lewd nakedness lurks beneath the man's raincoat. On the contrary, the gentleman is attired with perfect decency. Not richly, but tastefully. A navy blue suit with a vertical pinstripe, classically cut. The lapels on the jacket are wide, perhaps too wide for the lady's taste, but the carnation in the left button-hole, next to which the tip of a white handkerchief protrudes from the breast pocket, brings a momentary smile to her lips. But her face grows severe once more, she even frowns, when she notices the polka dots on his tie. They are discreet, not loud, a touch of lighter blue against the dark blue background, but what good is that when she doesn't care for polka dots? She hasn't since she was a little girl. It has to do with some childhood trauma of hers, something that cannot, for obvious reasons, be explained in any detail here. The stranger's shirt is blue too, in keeping with the general color-scheme.

The interior of his raincoat, however, is something out of the ordinary. Instead of a lining, which would not have been entirely inappropriate despite the warm, Indian-summer weather, the raincoat has several rows of wide, shallow pockets, running from the hem all the way up to the sleeves. A book, of varying size and thickness, is thrust into each pocket. There is a wide range of formats and cover designs. Some fifty titles in all. A veritable walking bookshop.

For several moments the lady pays no attention to the books, although she is aware of them. She is staring avidly into the gentleman's eyes—blue, of course—looming large through the magnifying lenses of his glasses, though they are in fact small and almost rodentlike. She seems to be trying to plumb the depths of his soul. Satisfied at last with what she sees there, she glances left, then right, to make sure nobody is about. On a fine day in the park there ought to be plenty of people with nothing better to do, but this episode requires a slight deviation from the laws of probability, for which no further justification is sought.

She untangles the leash from around her legs—bending down to do this, and keeping her knees straight, and she strokes the doggie for a moment: the doggie stops growling, even wags his tail a little; he could try standing on his hind legs a bit, but that would be overdoing it—and she moves near to the man. Now they are no more than one step apart. With a slow, caressing movement, the lady lifts the lace veil over the brim of her hat. Only now do we discover that she is wearing dark glasses, with frames like two beech leaves joined at the stem.

Before pulling her glasses halfway down her nose, she

The Book

licks her lips, first the upper, then the lower one. Traces of lipstick remain on her teeth, imparting a mildly mischievous effect. She begins to examine the books over the rim of her sunglasses, but for this she has to get really close to them, because she is short-sighted. Minus four in her right eye, minus two in her left. If that is the case, one might well ask why she doesn't wear proper glasses? But that would be impertinent, of course: it's not for us to explore a lady's hidden motives.

She scans the books unhurriedly, so as not to overlook any of the titles. The man, who is well-experienced, endures this inspection stoically. He exercises daily, he can do up to a hundred and twenty-six push-ups, so he can keep his arms spread for a long time. His head is raised, he gazes into the blue distances. In no way does he distract his customer, especially not by coughing. He is a consummate professional!

The lady slowly crouches down before him, then straightens up. Then down again. She performs this movement as many times as she scans the columns of books. Her close-fitting overcoat of lightweight pink gabardine stretches tight when she is in the lowest position. The cute little canine stands to one side, but wags his tail no longer. When she is finally done, the doggie's mistress retreats, but not by much, by maybe half a step at most. She first replaces her glasses, then drops her veil over her face. Finally, she smooths the wrinkles from the sides of her raincoat. By now there is no sign or trace of what she has just been doing. And it is at this moment that the gentleman allows himself the liberty of a level, rather than an upward gaze.

The lady does not make her decision immediately; such is the time-honored privilege of her class and gender. She places her right arm horizontally across her waist. With three fingers of her left hand she supports her chin, and leans back slightly: this is the politest thinking pose. The gentleman displays admirable pa-

54

tience; neither by word, gesture nor expression does he attempt to hurry her.

At long last she extends a hand, hesitates a little and selects a book. It may be possible to reveal which title she takes, but such excessive indiscretion cannot be justified. Suffice it to say that the bookmark is of pigeon-grey silk ribbon, the binding of brown canvas with a barrel spine and two grooves flanking the title. From this the cognoscenti will know which book it is.

The lady quickly puts the book in her handbag. It is, needless to say, pink in color and rather small, but somehow the book fits because it isn't thick. You'd scarcely guess, but the lady has a horror of thick volumes. She carefully considered this, among other things, when making her choice.

What happens next must be described with especial delicacy. By now our only remaining readers ought to be, as distinctly recommended, completely open-minded adults who may reasonably be expected not to blanch at human behavior, who are in fact prepared to encounter depths of depravity beyond the capacity of the most stalwart human. Yet numerous scruples demand that we maintain a civil tone as our narrative unfolds. Sad and sometimes bitter as it inevitably is, it is by no means intended to shock or horrify.

To that end, we must first take up the appropriate position. We will join the doggie, behind his mistress's back. We realize that this is entirely contrary to the etiquette of polite society; ladies must not be approached from behind in this manner, publicly and in broad daylight. But in our defense we plead that this way we opt for the lesser of two evils.

The doggie took refuge just here the moment he saw the book slide into the lady's handbag. The poor creature knows from experience what is about to happen. He even shuts his eyes, he even shields them with his ears. (This finally enables us to establish that he is not a poodle after all; it's common knowledge that poodles do not have long ears. By force of logic, this must be a miniature dachshund or something of the kind.)

We, of course, will not follow his example. Primarily because we, like poodles, do not have long ears (although in that regard, it's true, our somatotypes do vary). Also because if we covered our eyes we would see nothing, and thus ruin the opportunity to satisfy our avid but unseemly eagerness to know all (this being, by now, our principle motivation, loath as we might be to admit it).

So: first the lady sticks the handle of her frilly parasol in her pocket, in order to have that hand free. The sky is quite cloudless, and the sun benign; yet she has brought the parasol (which doubles as an umbrella) less for reasons of prudence (although the weather has been known to turn suddenly, especially in autumn) than because the parasol, which is also pink, completes her ensemble for walking in the park. Besides, it is small and no trouble to carry.

There has been no mention of the parasol until now because there was no need. It is but one of a whole range of similar bits and pieces that, for the same reason, will not be mentioned, despite the fact that they are delightful, charming, and above all useful—in short, very handy for describing or at least mentioning. But there's no point in agonizing over this, such is the nature of story-telling. One of the pitfalls of the profession.

What the lady does next, we can only infer. We can see she is using the fingers of both hands for some purpose down the front of her raincoat; the blinking and heavy breathing of the gentleman who still enjoys the privilege of a full-frontal view of developments (which we have willingly abjured) clearly indicate to us that something exciting, or more than exciting, is about to take place. At one point, as this business with the fingers is going on, he inserts a couple of his own fingers under his shirt collar to loosen it. It's got too tight for him, he is short of air. A few drops of sweat even appear on his forehead.

At last, everything becomes clear, even to us from our vantage-point behind the lady's back. The fingerwork was nothing more than the unbuttoning of her raincoat, believe it or not. With one sweep the lady opens the raincoat wide, and a huge pink sail unfurls in front of us, the umbrella dangling from one pocket, the purse hanging on one sleeve. The doggie, his eyes still tightly closed, hears the flapping rustling sound and knows precisely what has occurred; as a consequence he produces a thin keening noise—so sad, so poignant that it must surely touch the heart of even the hardest human.

There is no way for us to know exactly what spectacle is now vouchsafed to the gentleman with the curiously lined raincoat. To judge by his bulging eyes and slackened jaw, it must be something entirely out of the ordinary. Most likely we will never get the chance to enquire, however circumspectly, what it is he saw— conscious as we are that it might be very awkward for us and him alike—because, after staring for only a few moments, he starts suddenly as though waking from some spell, and half-strides, half-runs away. Without speaking a word. There has been, all in all, very little dialogue in this scene.

The lady also makes a swift exit, dexterously buttoning up her raincoat, smoothing it here and there, before retrieving the umbrella from her pocket. Then she turns, reaches down with her perforated pink gloves, and hugs the doggie, who is still shielding his eyes with his ears. By now the doggie is emitting a muffled sound, half a smothered bark and half a whimper. She starts whispering to him, soothing him, and twice she even draws him to her lips and kisses him lightly on the tip of his moist little nose.

If she ever noticed the presence of someone else behind her, she didn't show it.

*(From this point on, readers of all ages and moral scru-
ples are welcomed back, despite the fact that we are now
about to discuss a subject which has not until recently been
aired in public, or at least, not among polite society: conception. Of course, no living creature can describe from
experience how he or she was conceived. We, the books,
are no exception in this regard. The only witnesses to the
conception of books are, regrettably, humans, so we have
no recourse but to rely on their testimony. Not to worry,
though. Strict instructions have been issued to the human
narrator who will now, for a time, continue this treatise.
He has been told how to conduct himself, and in particular, what vocabulary to use, in order to avoid all trace of
that obscenity and bad taste which, among humans, almost invariably prevail when they discuss how life begins.)*

There is surely no area in which humans and books
differ more widely than in their manner of creating
new individuals. Most of the coarse and indecent terms
their languages contain refer to that supremely responsible and momentous act. In stark contrast to the vul-
garity and rudeness with which humans talk about it,
the act itself is performed in the greatest intimacy, often with much tenderness, and preferably in the dark,
so that, strictly speaking, not even the participants are
eyewitnesses to what they are doing.
With books it is exactly the opposite: open discussion of their manner of conception has always been
acceptable, even in the most puritanical of circles. No-
one has ever blushed or felt embarrassed about it. Even
the Church, by special decree, long ago declared this
act to be completely sinless. And the deed is done publicly, with numerous participants and witnesses, and of
necessity in strong lighting, without which it could not

be properly completed. Whoever heard of a book being made in the dark?

There are, however, some similarities between men and books as regards the continuation of the species. In both, the motive is by and large instinctive. How else could it be? Humans and books are branches of the same evolutionary tree. In both, the instinct is stronger in the male. Nature, for inscrutable reasons, has decreed it so. Ask any woman and she will confirm, from her own experience, that every male is obsessed with the drive to increase the human race by a little more—as if there weren't already far too many humans!

They're faced with overpopulation, the environment is polluted to dangerous levels, the ozone hole-and-a-half gapes hugely. Desert oases have dried up, while elsewhere everything is flooded. Earthquakes, tornadoes and tsunamis are on the increase all over the world, avalanches crash down even in midsummer, global warming is now unstoppable while in the meantime a new ice age is imminent, wars small and great break out in every region, a comet is about to slam into the planet, and to top it off, an invasion of evil aliens is every day expected.

What's more, the threat of shortages looms over mankind. It is harder and harder to find still mineral water, or mountain air in the cities, or electricity at summer rates, gas-canisters with working valves, lighter-fuel, fortified cod-liver oil, soya flour, cheesecakes, alcohol-free beer, ginger, mint tea, flaked tuna, early vegetables, powdered milk, salt 'n' vinegar chips, eucalyptus flavor chewing-gum, salted pistachios, steamed bagels, hazelnut chocolate—and people have forgotten what *tiramisu* even looks like.

There's also an unprecedented scarcity of studio flats, attics, bedsits, laundries, sheds, garages, basements, conservatories, tree-houses, workers' hostels, bothies and shanties. Not to mention that all the spaces in drive-in cinemas, supermarket car parks, pedi-cure salons, Olympic stadia, dentists' waiting-rooms, fast-food restaurants, underground trains, trade-union holiday resorts and nuclear shelters are booked solid for years to come. The world is covered with billboards, sometimes in flashing neon, shouting "Full!" or "Sold out!" but the good sirs, blinded like rabbits by their instinctive urges, want nothing more than to add to the population. They even take pride in their fecundity.

Were it not for an equally natural feminine restraint, were the females not holding back—though it doesn't come easy, instincts drive them too, even if less power-fully, at least while they are in charge of themselves and sober—and were it not for women's awareness that the responsibility for raising the subsequent offspring will fall mainly on their not very strong shoulders (one can scarcely rely, can one, on male help in this regard, on alimony or on child support)—the world would turn into one gigantic kindergarten, with adults wading knee-deep in babies.

It's much the same with publishing. Here the role of the insatiable male is filled by authors. Who else? And what's the use of telling them that there are already too many books in the world, that the whole place is crammed with them, libraries and bookshops are over-flowing, shelves terribly congested, warehouses and depots bulging like overstuffed suitcases, that every-thing has just about reached bursting-point? Restraint is unknown, there's long since been no sense of natural proportion. Utterly deaf are they to the voice of reason.

Fair enough, instinctive drives are innate, that's un-derstandable, but in this day and age there are con-traceptives available. Let authors write all they want if it makes them happy, no-one begrudges them it, but let them use a condom; not all writing must lead to the birth of a book. But no, mere pleasure isn't enough for these chaps, it isn't the real thing. The pleasure is worthless if the fruit of their masculinity isn't put on display for all and sundry. It must be a book. Without a book they don't feel they've achieved anything.

Publishing houses (which in many languages are also of the feminine gender) have a very hard time defending themselves from these assaults. It's not always a question of honor; sometimes the relationship may be legitimate. But what about the responsibility, the obligations? Authors have it easy. They potter about for a while until they've assembled a complete manuscript; rather a simple task, and one they enjoy—why would they do it otherwise and even call it, with typical male cynicism, by the proud name of "creativity"? But once they have done the deed, nearly all responsibility for giving birth and for the book's subsequent fate falls on the unfortunate publishing house, which has only its own resources to rely on.

Some publishing houses have been ruined in the long run by their excessive soft-heartedness towards authors. Sometimes, in their bitterness, you hear those destitute females remark that the life of a publishing house would be ideal if it didn't have to publish any books at all. Since there's no perfect contraceptive pill, they say, the best available solution is to be infertile. Then you can flirt with the authors to your heart's content, you can get into all sorts of adventures with them, be as promiscuous as you please; you can indulge all your feminine desires without fear of any consequences. No sexually transmitted diseases here, AIDS is out of the picture. The worst that can happen is a bit of gossip behind your back, but the tattletales in question are merely the envious petite-bourgeoisies who would be only too pleased to take your place if they could.

The other possibility, for those who are under genuine moral constraint, is to take refuge in a convent. Point blank refusal to have anything to do with authors. Under any circumstances. This is the most foolproof way to avoid an unwanted publishing pregnancy. Admittedly, not even the highest convent walls can save you from your natural urges, since the urges remain inside you, but there are well-tried and tested measures for smothering and suppressing such instinctual drives: regular prayer, long fasts, ice-cold showers, a vow of silence, kneeling on ears of grain in the corner of one's cell, frequent flagellation and—most challenging of all—abstinence from TV.

If all this does not help the nun to expel the authors from her head, and she continues to be obsessed and oppressed by them, if they persecute her in dreams, threatening her with their hard, swollen manuscript folders, then it is imperative that she confess to the abbess, who will urgently apply the ultimate means of spiritual rescue available: an exorcism.

Unfortunately the ritual is deeply unpleasant, even painful, and success is not guaranteed. Should it turn out that the Devil has taken up permanent residence inside this nun, and that she is lost to the Church forever, she has no other option but to face her grim destiny: her proper place is not in a convent at all, but rather in the sinful, corrupt, infamous world of authors, whither she must return as soon as possible lest her sinful thoughts divert from the righteous path any of the pure souls resident in that monastic haven.

The grievances of struggling publishing houses are understandable, nevertheless, their proposal really cannot be accepted. Where, indeed, would we be if all the publishing houses were to cease bringing books into the world? They would fail in their basic biological purpose. The species must be maintained: that is the bedrock of evolution! Of course, things should be organized in as civilized a way as possible; it must be known what is desirable and permitted, there must be strict rules of behavior, no concession must be made to the blind forces of chaos. Democracy is, of course, a given.

Experience has shown that publishing houses can best protect themselves from pushy authors by means of an intermediary service, one that has worked very successfully from time immemorial among humans but was imprudently abandoned under the guise of supposed emancipation: the matchmaker. In days of old it was unthinkable that a lad should go off alone to woo a bride for himself. Heaven forfend! The girl's father, if at all mindful of his own honor, would instantly throw such a young man out on his ear, no matter how eligible and no matter how much the girl loved him. Love was not a factor, not in the least. Some modicum of custom had to be respected.

It's true there were occasional instances in which the parents' wishes were defied, some elopements and abductions, some pre-marital affairs; even illegitimate children from time to time. Why deny it, human nature being what it is? It's thanks to this permissiveness and disorder that there are now six billion humans on this poor planet, this wretched celestial orb now groaning and buckling under the burden of its myriad inhabitants; all living creatures on Earth suffer the consequences.

No, each young fellow intent on marriage had to engage the services of a matchmaker. There was no other way. The matchmaker would arrange everything: approach the young lady's household, where he would be graciously received; inform her father of the honorable intentions of his client whose qualities and prospects he would, of course, unrealistically extol, particularly those qualities which cannot be readily verified, let alone quantified: honesty, goodness, nobility of soul, industry and general benevolence. This was all the easier since no actual guarantees were expected.

The offer being accepted, the parties would commence the process of arranging the various technical and financial details, primarily the dowry. This was particularly important because, by an unwritten rule, commission for the matchmaker's invaluable services was ten percent of the dowry, which meant that he was very powerfully motivated indeed to obtain the maximum sum in his negotiations.

The profession of matchmaking was considered highly respectable. The matchmaker was, in fact, one of the pillars of society, on a par with the priest, the mayor, the chief of police, the midwife, the barber, the postmaster, the apothecary, the innkeeper, the fire chief, the commander of the local garrison, the sexton, the teacher, the vet and the directors of the opera and ballet. All doors were open to him, there was not a celebration, whether private or public, to which he was not invited.

Not all human machinations merit disapproval: some of them are not entirely without virtue. Besides, in human affairs the best indicator of the value of something is its abandonment. Publishing houses did wisely when they embraced the discarded matchmaking service. With all due respect to progress in general and emancipation in particular, this was a case of defending the publishers' very existence against a deadly infestation of authors. By any means possible.

The name could not be kept, however. Something more in accord with modern sensibilities had to be invented, something that would not evoke traces of an unsophisticated past; a dignified, serious title, in keeping with the importance of such a profession. After a number of misfires, one name finally achieved general and permanent acceptance: the publishing matchmaker was dubbed the "literary agent." Elegant and to the point.

Only in the most backward societies do publishing houses still condescend to expose themselves to the huge and unnecessary unpleasantness of directly associating with authors. In the civilized world, only a young, totally inexperienced beginner would send his manuscript directly to a publisher. The envelope will soon be returned to him, unopened, but accompanied by a curt rejection slip, to the effect that any repetition of his rude inconsiderate behavior will result in his being blacklisted for life throughout the publishing profession. Harsh treatment, to be sure, but quite necessary. Everyone knows how juvenile delinquents must be dealt with, and it leaves no room for sentimentality. If you let them get away with it the first time, next time will be far more serious.

Only in a chilly postscript, in the small print usually reserved for legal disclaimers, will the suggestion be made that he might seek advice from a literary agent. Mortified by his *faux pas*, but still blinded by a great longing to see his offspring published, the young writer will set off in search of a member of that profession and send the manuscript to him, hoping that, even if he doesn't find a publisher quickly, he may at least get a speedy and unbiased reader's report. But now a second unpleasant surprise awaits him: he has no idea how difficult and pressurized the life of a literary matchmaker is.

He least of all has time to devote himself to reading manuscripts, even if he wanted to. And no wonder. How could he have, with all the other obligations weighing down on him? To begin with, he must write innumerable letters, faxes, telegrams, emails, memos, writs, proposals, contracts, addenda, bills, invoices, warnings, catalogues, statements, denials, articles, checks, tax reports, diary entries and unattributable briefings to the police. Then there is conversation through at least two telephone lines simultaneously (one phone has to be a mobile, that's mandatory) while three other lines (at least one of them international) are on hold. Then an unbroken stream of meetings and at least three daily business lunches, plus an occasional business snack if there is a contact with a large appetite that day. Add to this the visits to book fairs, conventions, festivals, biennials, exhibitions, presentations, promotions, book-launches, ceremonial openings and closings, village fetes and other professional gatherings which would be blighted without his personal presence—and it becomes quite clear that he has no time for reading.

Luckily, reading is not part of the art. Why should it be? His forbear never wasted time getting to know the lad he was going to recommend. The real qualities (or absence thereof) of the prospective bridegroom mattered not at all. The point of the matchmaker's art was to sell a pig in a poke. Of course, the absence of glaring faults was an advantage, but not essential. In the hands of a truly skillful matchmaker, failings became virtues and virtues took on an almost supernatural luster. You had to earn your ten percent by some really hard salesmanship. And once the deal was done, no subsequent objections would be entertained.

The most that a youthful writer could hope for, having sent his manuscript to a reputable agent, was that the agent might agree to represent him. This was a rare favor, and should it be bestowed upon the fledgling author, he could consider himself extraordinarily lucky and privileged. It was almost as good as winning the lottery jackpot, and only a little more likely. Moreover it meant half the job was done. The rest was more or less a technicality.

The manuscript would then be recommended, in carefully chosen words and in a highly ceremonious atmosphere, most likely over lunch in some expensive restaurant. There, among the liveried waiters, with candlelight twinkling off the champagne and caviar, its virtues would be expounded to the director of the publishing house, standing in here for the father of the girl. The fact that the agent had only a vague, general and often entirely mistaken idea of his client's work was no hindrance at all, because nothing hinged on the manuscript's actual character. Everything depended on its presentation, in which the promotional and marketing talent of the matchmaker would play a key role.

To a naive onlooker it might seem that the agent's hype would be assisted by a certain gullibility on the part of the director. One would not expect a director to accept a manuscript purely on an agent's recommendation, however eloquent and persuasive it may be. It might seem to a prudent person that the director should be especially wary, precisely because the offer was so hyped. At the very least, the director should read the thing, and thereby obtain, quite quickly, a clear insight into the realities of the case.

Any such expectation would be based on a total unfamiliarity with certain aspects of the directorial role. It is not widely known, but the directors of tobacco companies are passionate non-smokers. Likewise, all directors of distilleries are sworn teetotalers. In the same spirit, directors of publishing houses are rigidly opposed to the bad habit of reading. They don't object if other people read—not at all. How else would they make money? But they are careful of their own health and wellbeing; and who can blame them for that?

Besides, reading serves no purpose. What is to be gained by it? At worst, the director might discover that the manuscript was not as good as the agent implied, or even that it was completely meretricious, but this would not hinder its being published, and for two reasons. First, an advance has already been paid; second, the contract that the agent will soon sign on the author's behalf will contain an important caveat to the effect that the publisher has free rein to adjust the manuscript according to his own needs.

Editors are those who do the creative work of adjustment. They are the true wizards of the publishing trade. There is nothing they cannot accomplish. To begin with, they follow the trends. They are well-informed about demand in bookshops, they know the readers' tastes. If, for example, the fashion is for fast-moving erotic thrillers, and if the manuscript they have received for adjustment happens to concern the chaste and serene goings-on of a medieval convent, with a wealth of exhaustive theological discussion (elaborately foot-noted for the full benefit of the layperson), the editor will perceive this vast discrepancy only as a challenge commensurate with his skill.

His creative adjustment completed, the innocent monastery will have become a hotbed of various unhallowed passions, with sodomy predominant. Meanwhile, the drowsy monotony of monastic life will have turned into a thrilling rollercoaster of exciting, gruesome and supremely horrifying adventures, centered on the activities of an ingeniously sadistic serial killer, this being the type of protagonist with which the reading public most easily identifies.

From the purely technical point of view, editors will respect the two principles which guarantee a smooth and easy read. There must be as much dialogue as possible, without unnecessary descriptions which would slow the plot down; and the longest paragraphs must never extend beyond five lines. It has been scientifically proven that five lines represent the limit of the average reader's attention span, and he must be continually catered to because he is the bedrock of long print-runs. You can't make a living out of those weird loners who despise dialogue and go in for long paragraphs.

The author learns of all these adjustments only after the book is in the shops. It's no doubt a shock to him; the man may not be able to recognize the text as his, but his initial anger will quickly dissipate.

For a start, here is his dream made solid in his hand: a published book, with his name on the cover. What's more, the royalties are coming in; not nearly as high as he imagined in his wilder moments, but welcome all the same. Lastly, he may come to prefer the edited version, and forget from then on that there was ever any adjustment. Besides, no mention is made of it on the publisher's imprint page. The man adroitly persuades himself that no changes were ever made to the original manuscript. He is, in fact, surprised to see how good a writer he actually is.

At this juncture you might reasonably ask: Why start with the author's original, if ultimately there's almost nothing left of it? Wouldn't it be simpler just to let the editor write the whole thing, as at the end of the day he did? The point is well made, but the person who raised it would only be demonstrating his complete unfamiliarity with the nature of human affairs, whereby questions of ease and simplicity are seldom—if ever—regarded.

There is one further consideration which absolves the director from the tortuous obligation of reading the manuscript to discover how good or bad it really is. Even if there were no caveat about adjustment to the publisher's needs, and even if the manuscript were published exactly as it stood, sales would still remain quite unaffected. This is because books have one other wondrous attribute: the purchaser can't see and judge their value with quite the ease he can when, for example, he buys a pair of shoes.

To ascertain the value of a book, you must first read it, and to read it, you must of course first purchase it. There's no way round this, if we discount some occasional and quite illegal exceptions. And once the book has been bought, all regret is futile. No bookshop will make a refund simply because the buyer doesn't like a book. Not even a shoe shop, in fact, will replace a pair of shoes if the customer returns a few days later and says they are uncomfortable.

Buying a book is not, however, buying a pig in a poke, although it might seem so. The customer's decision is not entirely blind; various indicators are there to assist him. The book's thickness, to begin with. It's true that in these modern times people have less and less time to read, yet an ancient, pre-TV belief persists that thick books are somehow worth more than thin ones—if for no other reason than the larger quantity of paper they contain. Weighing up in his hands a fat volume and a lean one, the customer always feels his heart incline towards the heftier of the two. It strikes him as more concrete, more palpable, more of a handful, as the saying goes.

Next, the look of the thing. This is very important. We live in an age when the sale of goods depends largely on packaging. A book in a shiny jacket with an embossed title, a colorful and startling illustration (including perhaps a mildly erotic element) will grab the buyer's attention much more readily than a book with a drab, monochrome cover, no matter what the subject matter of the two books may be. In olden days there was a proverb to the effect that a book should not be judged by its cover, but that proverb was abandoned long ago.

There are, however, some intelligent individuals among the buying public, who won't decide solely on thickness and appearance. No, they go by something more reliable. They like to read, for instance, the blurb on the back of the jacket or the flaps, outlining what the book is about. Not a complete summary, it wouldn't do to give away the denouement, but a synopsis stating the main gist of the plot is a convenient aid to making the right choice. Not everyone likes the same kind of story.

A plot summary by itself is, however, not always enough. How should one choose between two very similar plots? A cautious buyer, one who is determined not to be caught out, has one oracle to rely on in such dilemmas: the opinion of experts. In other words, the review extracts taken from respectable newspapers and magazines and prominently printed on the book. These carry far more weight than the publishers' blurbs. They are something like a guarantee, or seal of quality.

The sales of a book also indicate its quality. If two books are competing head-to-head, and if they are similar in every respect except that one has a smaller print-run than the other, or only one edition, a wise buyer will always choose the latter. Moreover, he will prefer the one with the higher position on the bestsellers list. In both cases the customer will be governed by this infallible logic: so many people can't all be wrong!

And for the most discerning who want nothing but the best, the only real recommendation is a reputable book award. Nothing less will interest them. The moment they step into a bookshop, the first thing they go in search of is that strip of paper known as a banderole, wound tightly around a book's middle to announce which award the book has won. The banderole even resembles a prize-ribbon, or the sash belonging to a high order of chivalry—which is how a token of high quality ought to look. An announcement of the award may also be printed on the corner of the front cover, in which case it's made to resemble a triangular medal, also quite appropriate.

Of course, the director has all these circumstances in mind when he buys a manuscript from an agent. Instead of wasting his time reading the thing, he will wisely maneuver into place all the elements that will really determine sales. The value of the text itself is quite irrelevant.

If the manuscript isn't long enough, there are at least three methods of padding it out. Thicker paper is one; halfway to being cardboard in fact, like in children's picture-books, so that a hundred pages will give the same impression as three hundred on regular paper. Additionally, there is no theoretical limit to the size of the font and equally unrestrained freedom as to the width of the margins; plus lots of blank, empty pages wherever there is an opportunity to insert them. People generally like a fast read, and there are plenty who can't see small type very well, so this is good for them. Finally, illustrations may be used, perhaps in color, and may be slapped across entire pages. Their purpose is twofold: the reader will rest his eyes, tired from gazing at text, and he will also discover whether he has imagined the events and places properly. These procedures swiftly transform a mid-length novella into a doorstop novel.

The graphic designer then gets down to work. There's no need for him, either, to discover in detail what the book is about; a hint of the contents will be enough for him to produce a cover illustration so nebulous it may even be used on the text it was ordered for. The basic requirements, in any case, are lots of bright colors along with plenty of action, a loud title and obligatory nudity. The extent of the nudity varies, however, depending on the kind of novel: the most revealing will be found on books of a melodramatic nature, though it won't stray beyond the barriers of good taste. In other words, it won't extend to pornography: a naked female neck and shoulders may suffice. For religious and metaphysical essays the bare flesh will be kept to a minimum; for these a slightly raised petticoat with a lace trim, revealing no more than a glimpse of calf, may do.

The plot summary for the jacket presents something of a problem, since the person composing it needs to have at least some remote idea of what the book is about. This summary really shouldn't describe a totally different book, though this has been known to happen and to pass unnoticed. A skillful editor, however, will phrase a summary in such general terms that no-one will notice that he doesn't actually enjoy a very close familiarity with the contents. Writing like this is not that difficult to produce. Clichés applicable to various types of narrative, and especially to genre fiction, have long been in circulation. It's basically a matter of changing the names, the rest comes pre-packaged, only requiring assembly. Genres are God's gift to editors, who have better things to do than read swathes of redundant prose.

As for blurbs, the solution is twofold. First of all, any serious publisher can get a critic to be positive. Exactly how he does so is a trade secret, naturally. The details are under wraps, but by all accounts, it isn't very hard. It's surprising how willing and eager literary critics can be, if approached in the right way. But isn't this true of many other professions?

The publisher makes every effort to accommodate a friendly critic. To begin with, he gives them an advance copy of the book so that the review can appear in the press before the book has actually been published; how else could it be quoted on the cover? This is the proper order of events, though it isn't always abided by, since there have been cases when a book appears thus endorsed, and the review quoted comes out considerably later—or never; but why split hairs? After a certain interval none of it will matter anyway. It's an academic question, surely—like the chicken and the egg?

Besides, the publisher doesn't absolutely require that the reviewer should actually read the work presented to him for review. In a civilized business such as this, both sides will take it for granted that the reviewer has done his job properly. No-one is going to demand proof. What kind of an attitude would that be? Only the author, in fact, would be in a position to make such a demand, because he is the only person, thus far in the publishing process, who can be relied upon to have read the manuscript (though there are exceptions even to this). But the author wouldn't dream of intruding in this manner. It would be a nasty surprise for him if, having read a glowing review of his book, he subsequently discovered that the reviewer hadn't in fact the foggiest idea of what it was he had praised.

There are also a few reviewers whose powerful integrity does not permit them to hobnob with publishers. Some of these even refuse the free copy issued to reviewers as of right. They simply won't be bribed: they walk into a bookshop, take out their wallet and purchase the book in question, even though it may cost them more than their fee for the review. They value their independence highly, considering it a guarantee of objective impartiality. And however we choose to regard their fiercely idealistic stance, one thing has to be said for this unique breed of critics: they, at least, will have read the book.

Which is the main source of trouble. Had the Devil let them live in peace, had they, like everyone else, just skipped the reading, they wouldn't have reason to pass their (usually very negative) judgment. The publisher, of course, has no use for their negativity, which he has done nothing to provoke, so he must hit on some devious means of neutralizing its effect. His usual strategy is to ignore it. As the proverb says: No miracle lasts longer than three days. Hardly anybody reads newspaper articles, and of those who do, no-one remembers them long.

A clever publisher, though, can turn even a bad review to his advantage. It isn't really such a difficult trick: adroit handling will convert the harshest criticism into praise. Let us assume the reviewer has concluded with a clear statement: "This novel sets a new standard for disastrous failure!" The publisher will not hesitate to print this on the back of the gleaming dust-jacket, in bold letters, even, to lend it added prominence. Nor will it be altered—not at all. The overblown sentence will just be edited slightly, to fit the available space, something the publisher is surely entitled to do. Scientists do as much in their research papers, only quoting the essential parts. "This novel sets a new standard!" An accurate quotation of the critic's words? Of course it is.

Another way of measuring a book's success is by the number of editions it has gone through. The more the better, needless to say. This is why no publisher starts with the first. Why quibble? The very first copies to roll off the printing presses will proudly bear the legend: "Fourth edition!" This is usually emblazoned on a thickly-framed gold star, the better to attract the attention of potential buyers. The only person skeptical enough to investigate its veracity would be some determined bibliophile bent on assembling a complete collection, with first, second and third editions all represented. No matter how much money he's prepared to offer he will remain eternally frustrated. But who takes any notice of the doubts of frustrated bibliophiles?

It's a great advantage promotionally if some previous work by the same author has reached the bestsellers list, a recommendation which will surely be printed prominently on the dust-jacket. It won't be missed off, even for the very first book by a brand new author. In such circumstances, it will be patently absurd, but it can be phrased so that hardly anyone will notice the absurdity. Few people pay attention to the finer points of logic, and there's no doubt the announcement is a head-turner: "The first book by the very famous writer of countless bestsellers!"

Similarly, it will prove profitable to claim that the new work has achieved bestsellerdom even before its first publication. If the previous claim is taken into account, as it must be, then this is the logical conclusion: how could this be the fourth edition, if the first three had not totally sold out? Consistency and above all, a rational approach: these have always been essential to the publishing trade.

Awards caused some publishers headaches in the early days. It was at this point that a cast-iron, essentially risk-free business was penetrated and endangered by a loose cannon: namely, the whims and caprices of juries. Naturally, this had to be put a stop to. Just think of all the money and effort a publisher must invest to publish a book, only to have it denigrated and ruined by some idle jury who says it is not to their taste! Just imagine! As if anybody cares what a jury likes or dislikes! And who are these people, anyway, pronouncing such awful judgments?

That was the key question, and moreover, the solution to the problem. Studying the matter a little more closely, the publishers discovered, to their relief, that members of literary juries are not such ogres as they might at first appear. Quite the opposite, in fact: it turned out that they, just like critics, are most kindly, genial people, almost without exception ready to co-operate in various ways.

Besides, members of literary juries have an important quality, one they share with almost all the other links in the long publishing chain: their dislike of reading. What's more, this quality is more pronounced in their case than with others in the chain, and understandably so. A superhuman feat of endurance is expected of the jury members, namely, to wade through an entire ocean of published material, because only in this way is it possible to choose the best. If they were literally to fulfill this obligation, they would have to spend their entire waking lives reading, and even that would probably not be enough. What living creature would not, as a result, become nauseated with reading, no matter how much he or she might have liked it at first?

Luckily, shortcuts have been discovered along this

thorny path. As it turns out, there are several ways to get a reliable impression of a book without having to read it line by line in what we might term the "classical" sense. The first to be invented was the so-called "diagonal reading" technique. No-one can quite explain what it consists of, or how it is done, but many people use diagonal reading successfully, just as many people drive cars successfully without having so much as an inkling of how the internal combustion engine actually works. Is it really crucial to know how a thing functions, if it functions well? Diagonal reading reduced from five minutes to about ten seconds the time needed to read an average page.

Skipping proved to be an even more effective technique, and gained its justification from the fact that writers are notorious for their tendency to overwrite, embellish, meander and digress. They also overdo the descriptive passages, add superfluous episodes and other redundant material, pile on the adjectives and whitter on about their hobbies and hang-ups; so you don't miss out on anything essential if you restrict your reading to the odd-numbered pages—or even to every fifth page. A speedier version of this method, whereby one's eyes fall only upon every tenth page, enables one to vanquish even a thick volume in under an hour—an undeniable improvement.

But it was only with the leafing-through technique that reading really caught up with the pace of modern life. This allowed a jury member to gain insight into the specified book in just a few minutes, insight deep enough for him to discuss that book anywhere, on the spur of the moment, and even to enter into passionate if abstruse debate over the finer points of detail. If, for instance, a person was so incautious as to maintain that the book was dull, the juror would be able to oppose that statement with the rejoinder that no book could be dull when it was so stuffed with dialogue. He knew this for certain, having seen the dialogue passages with his own eyes; they were impossible to overlook, even with the fastest page-turning.

Genuinely busy jury members, those who don't even have time to leaf through, must rely on so-called "indirect techniques," though they aren't as reliable as direct techniques. This involves reading the summary on the back flap of the dust-wrapper, but owing to the vague, generalized character of such passages, it doesn't teach one much. Some jury members do settle for this, however, applying the foolproof dictum that "something is better than nothing." Nor can their logic be faulted. The hard-working types who actually read the summary must surely know more about the book than those who did not.

Despite the fact that it may seem dangerously unreliable, the technique most favored by jury members and the most frequently used, is the one we might call "straight from the horse's mouth." First and foremost, this represents a great saving of those two most precious commodities: time and effort. To make effective use of it you need only be good at knowing and contacting people—as every serious juror ought to be. If he doesn't know and contact many people, he has no business being appointed to a position of such weighty responsibility.

All that's required is to go out and mingle socially with those idle types who have nothing much to do, or who just happen to be the sort of weirdos who will actually have read the book in question. Then you deftly persuade them to talk about it. This will require little prompting; such people love to brag about their great achievements. Thus, in no time at all, you can gather as much information as you like about the book in question, and what's more, you can adopt a firm opinion about it. That's no minor matter when it comes to voting, because in this way justice is most satisfactorily served. Although indirectly, a judgment based on actual reading decides which book will get the award. What result could be more appropriate?

It was only in the early days that publishers had serious trouble, when there was just one big award, the Grand Prize. From this it followed that all the other books had to go without. As this was an extremely inequitable arrangement, it was obvious that in order to achieve greater fairness a more democratic system would have to be worked out.

First, as an interim measure, a consolatory "honorable mention" was introduced into the process of competition for the Grand Prize. Observers shadowed the jury work closely, and the jury was supposed gradually to whittle the field down. This sifting process was in itself very handy for promotional purposes. Even an announcement of the initial list of candidates brought profit. Although this longlist includes all the entrants for the competition, because, strictly speaking, no choosing or selecting has yet taken place, banderoles soon appeared on many books, proudly stating: "A Contender for the Grand Prize!" A mild improvement in sales immediately resulted.

After the longlist came, of course, the not-quite-so-long list. A certain amount of confusion arose here at first, because the number of titles actually grew rather than shrank as might have been expected. But matters were soon clarified. Although some of the titles from the original list were dropped for various reasons, mostly because impatient publishers had entered them for the competition before the books were actually published, or even before they were written, other books popped up in the meantime which fulfilled all the requirements and therefore had to be placed on the list of competitors. This constant influx of new candidates for the Grand Prize would continue until the very moment at which the winner was announced, and sometimes even after the announcement. The banderoles that adorned the not-quite-so-long listed books were, as was fitting, of a somewhat more cheerful color.

Then the jury would get seriously chuffing away, gathering momentum, crashing through all the reading barriers, and the choice would be narrowed down even further, although the number of contenders for the Grand Award did not necessarily have to become smaller. The narrower choice was followed, inevitably, by "a choice a bit narrower still," then "a yet another bit narrower choice," then "a fairly narrow choice," "a narrow choice without special qualifiers," "a strictly narrow choice," "a limited narrow choice," "a very narrow choice," "a choice narrower than very narrow," then "trimmed down," and soon after the "slashed choice," followed by the "extremely narrow choice," the "narrowest possible choice," "impossibly narrow choice," "unbelievably narrowest choice," and ultimately, "the last one hundred and twenty-eight candidates with an option of increasing the number to one hundred and forty-three, if, at the last moment, works of special cultural and general social importance should appear." It goes without saying that with each mounting step towards the Grand Prize, the cheerfulness of the banderole colors increased, making the bookshop windows look like halls decked out for Christmas. Only the tinsel was missing.

As Judgment Day neared, the five jury members became the most sought-after persons on the planet. Imagine all the weird and wonderful methods that publishers and other interested parties made use of, in their attempts to contact and persuade them at the eleventh hour, by means honorable and otherwise, to support their candidate! Only the naive and inexperienced fell back on conventional approaches. At first the telephones of the magnificent five were continually busy. Then they were disconnected because of the huge overload on the central exchange. At its height there was even a danger of the entire network collapsing.

Postmen continued, for a while, to deliver the letters, postcards, picture-postcards, greetings cards, parcels and telegrams festooned with perfume and ribbons. These poor posties sweated and bowed under the increasing weight of mail, and when it finally passed all tolerable limits, the Postal Workers' Union demanded (and won) a restriction on delivery—for purely humanitarian reasons: they weren't mules, after all! Enough was enough! It was suggested to the gentlemen of the jury that, should they so wish, they might come along to the post office and pick up their mail from there.

This did nothing to abate the sundry attempts to contact jury members even after it was announced, in the most prominent slots in all the newspapers, that they would not be allowed to receive any visitors until after their deliberations were completed. Security men were stationed in front of their houses, prepared to frisk all comers. Determined visitors, however, resorted to incredible subterfuges. They materialized at the door disguised as all manner of meter-readers, veterinary or financial inspectors, drinks delivery-men, undertakers, Red Cross collectors, chimney-sweeps, plainclothes policemen, public opinion canvassers, priests sent to administer Extreme Unction, electricians, removal men, house-painters, paramedics and family members (whether close or distant).

In the end, the buildings in which the jurors were resident became subject to full border regulations. There would be a barrier at the entrance, metal detectors, luggage search, identity screening with fingerprint verification by police computer, and an extensive body search, including bacterial throat-swab. After that the tide of visitors ebbed somewhat; but, as is only to be anticipated in such exceptional circumstances, a number of secret channels began to open up, some obviously inspired by the world of espionage.

First it was noticed that an unusually large number

of pigeons were landing on the windowsills of jury members. These turned out to be messenger pigeons, though this title proved somewhat inappropriate since the cargoes they were expected to deliver, by their bulk and weight, went far beyond a pigeon's normal call of duty. Eventually a campaign against such abuse of the poor creatures was launched by the Association for the Protection of Feathered Animals. The Society for **~~the~~ the Preservation of City joined in the protest, because these large flocks of pigeons inevitably soiled, to an unacceptable degree, both the buildings and immediate surroundings.

Pigeons were not alone in flying to the innocent windows of the jury members. These windows became the targets for a concerted campaign of varied optical signaling. Sunny days found it possible to send messages by simple heliograph, from some nook across the street, using Morse, Braille, or some other code—into a bedroom, preferably, or if that could not be managed, into the dining room or at worst the kitchen. The bathroom was a last resort. An ignorant visitor might have been amazed by the frantic scintillation, reflection, blinking and refraction in and on the windows—even when closed, curtained and shuttered up.

At night the spectacle grew even more pyrotechnic. To begin with, numberless intermittent torch-beams roamed the windowpanes; in a later crescendo spotlights were brought in from somewhere, small at first, then larger, so that the jurors' apartment buildings glowed like palaces hosting great balls or receptions. These glittering light-shows were subsequently enhanced by lasers, whose slender beams adorned the windows with multicolored roaming points of light.

The boldest publishers did not balk or even blench at genuine commando-style raids, all for the sake of somehow accessing the elusive jurors before the last and decisive session. Generally speaking, two approaches were favored: above and below. If the neighboring buildings were of a similar height, it proved relatively easy to cross their roofs to the roof of the target building. A padlocked skylight, even the lack of one, was no serious obstacle to these well-drilled and even better motivated action heroes.

If there were differences in height, these were no problem either. On critical days there was, it seemed, an uncanny increase of interest among chimney-sweeps in the jurors' neighborhoods. This was, naturally, no more than an excuse to position tall ladders against the nearby buildings, the better to achieve the destined roof. Thereafter it was plain abseiling.

In special cases, when this could not be done, great feats of acrobatic skill were performed under cover of night: rappelling with mountaineering hooks up the facade, hurling a rope and grapnel, then climbing up, or walking an improvised tightrope from the building opposite, as often as not without the aid of a balancing pole. Eventually, if all else failed, various infantry landing techniques were employed. One fearless publisher almost got himself killed in an attempt to parachute from the top of a nearby tall building, while another caused an air traffic control incident when piloting a microlight towards the roof of one jury member.

Infiltration from below came mostly through the sewers. In order to facilitate this, publishers produced an unofficial guide through the underground city labyrinths, with specially highlighted diversions towards the homes of all those major cultural personalities who might sooner or later be expected to join the jury. This regularly updated memo was, of course, unavailable to the public.

The authorities having, for reasons of safety and public hygiene, taken steps to discourage these widespread practices, the publishers did not give up—far from it! Never underestimate a publisher's sheer dogged per-

sistence. Once the sewer access-tunnels under the jurors' buildings were officially sealed off, they had no
recourse but to begin digging other, secret tunnels, in
the best tradition of World War II escape movies. Fortunately jurors tend to stay put in the same apartments
for a number of years. So, once dug, an underground
corridor can be used on various occasions.

Meanwhile, the authorities didn't sit on their hands.
Once discovered, each shaft was immediately blocked
off, and if there was sufficient evidence to prove which
publisher had dug it, he was required to pay a hefty
fine, plus the cost of restoring the landscape to its previous condition (and associated making-good). He was
also ritually but publicly rebuked in the newspapers.
Yet none of this succeeded in deflecting the most en-
terprising from their intent. Finding their options limited, they began to think more soberly, and hit on a
simpler solution—though one requiring some advance
preparation.

A stitch in time saves nine. Infiltrate your man early
is the motto. In the language of spooks, such an op-
erator is known as a "mole." In the case of publishers,
some of them, unfortunately, took this term at first too
literally. A few installed their mole in the cellars of the
jury building as much as two and a half months before he was to be activated. The worst of it was not just
the agent's having to spend so much time in the cellar;
hiding under a coal-heap or a woodpile for so long is
not exactly a pleasurable experience, even if you are a
special forces agent inured to all sorts of hardships and
privations, and the fees paid for weeks of unproductive
suffering were set accordingly.

Some of the brighter luminaries in the publishing
constellation observed that this matter could be handled with more finesse. They procured for their mole
the position of inconspicuous janitor in the target
building. The mole was especially eager to offer the

juror prompt and efficient assistance of all kinds (free of charge, naturally) whenever something malfunctioned, broke down, got stuck or clogged up, fell off, came loose, unglued itself, leaked, got rained on, blistered up, scraped off, burnt out, fused, cracked, or went wrong in any other manner.

The mole was willing to help in other ways, far beyond a janitor's normal remit. He could tune the piano of the overworked juror, pick up his kids from kindergarten, install a new computer program, exercise the greyhounds, secure and re-orientate a loose satellite dish antenna, or clean the carburetor in the car. Whatever favor the jury member asked, the mole complied with a smile, the deeper to ensnare him in his moral debt. How else could the juror's benevolence be counted on, when it came to the decisive moment?

Fat-cat publishers, those for whom no expense was too great, opted for an even more elegant solution. Their mole was a respectable citizen who rented or even bought a flat in the same building, and tried, without provoking suspicion, to become first acquainted, then friendly, then very closely and intimately friendly with the juror, who had no inkling of the awesome web of conspiracy being woven around him. This was particularly easy to do if the mole was in the medical profession. Everyone likes to have a doctor friend on his doorstep; jury members are no exception—on the contrary.

Once the day dawned on which the Grand Prize must be decided, there could be no further possibility of influencing the robust impartiality of the jury members: whatever you'd achieved, you'd achieved, and that was that. At precisely ten o'clock in the morning, armored cars with spinning lights would pull up, amid a banshee wailing of sirens, at five addresses throughout the city. Crack units in bulletproof vests and combat helmets, their transparent visors down, weapons loaded and cocked, would surround the entrance to each apartment block and complete one last communications check with the lookouts and snipers positioned in nearby buildings and in low-hovering helicopters. They then rapidly led their charges out of the house and into the armored car. At the slightest sign of danger they were ready to throw themselves on the jury member, to protect him with their body like good bodyguards, and proceed to open fire mercilessly on the would-be assassin or terrorist.

Only the inner circle of the police force knew where all five armored cars were heading. That venue was top secret. The jurors would meet there, hermetically sealed from the outside world. The sole person allowed to come into contact with them was the waiter who brought them coffee and mineral water; cigarettes and alcohol were not formally forbidden, but neither were they provided free of charge, owing to potential misuse. The waiter himself was masked and forbidden to speak.

Rarely was this final meeting swift to finish. On the whole it was rather long—it would last, indeed, until one book received the necessary majority of three votes. But this was by no means easy to achieve, since the starting-point was always that no two members supported the same book; each had pledged undying loyalty to his own favorite. From this followed a tense period of sickeningly friendly negotiations, continuing for hours or even days.

There were no official reports of the atmosphere inside, but reasonably reliable rumors indicated that it was not unduly academic. The uniformed guards protecting the jury room occasionally heard, through the thick soundproofing, words and exclamations such as to cause raised eyebrows, hardboiled though they were by nature and training. Crashing and smashing sounds were sometimes heard, but as to the origin of these noises there was no credible explanation. The juries' deliberations might in some cases have lasted indefinitely, had it not been for one very strict rule. Under no circumstances could members leave the room until they had made their final decision. Not even medical exigency was respected. Jurors' physical wellbeing was ensured by a dedicated team armed with, among other things, resuscitation equipment. Although the initial idea was that this team should only be there on standby, "just in case," with no real responsibilities, events took a different course.

And contrary to expectations, only a small number of the interventions required related to the physical fatigue or nervous collapse that might be expected in such circumstances. Professional ethics prevented the doctors from publicizing details of their patients' conditions, but inferences could be drawn from their requisitions—which included copious quantities of plaster for casts, braces and suture thread.

In the end weariness, exhaustion, sleeplessness, and other factors that could only be glimpsed or guessed at broke (sometimes literally) certain of the least morally sound and physically sturdy jury members, although all had diligently honed themselves, mind and body, for a marathon session, as though intending to complete an Olympic decathlon. And now the winner of the Grand Prize was about to be announced.

The news was not reported first by the electronic media, in keeping with the spirit of modernity. For some reason, an archaic mode of communication was preferred: white smoke, billowing from the chimney of the chief sponsor's building, would proclaim that the laureate had been chosen.

From the moment the jury commenced their deliberations, restless devotees began gathering outside the building. Their numbers increased rapidly until all the available space was filled, as if for a big political demonstration. The old hands among the crowd would arrive prepared for a lengthy vigil. Individual rations consisted of: plentiful amounts of water or other refreshing drink; packets of dried or preserved food; an umbrella; a stool; and possibly a sleeping-bag—this last in case there should be no clear early leader in the race, which meant that the deliberations would be prolonged.

Everyone stared fixedly at the great chimney, for it was a source of much kudos to be the first to notice a sinuous white coil begin to snake from it. For some years, this signaled merely that a decision had been reached, not who had won. Then the organizers of the ceremony decided to correct that deficiency by making use of an even more ancient method of communication: the smoke signal. Instead of just letting the white smoke pour out of the chimney, they modulated it by a special procedure, so that it appeared in regulated puffs.

Only a few in the crowd possessed the rare literacy skills required in order to read the message growing from the chimney. Everyone else flocked eagerly around such individuals. Total silence reigned while they spelled it out, syllable by smoky syllable. Excitement grew gradually, since, as in a beauty contest, the winners were announced from the bottom up, rather than from the top down. First the twenty-fifth place was proclaimed, then the twenty-fourth, and so on till the runner-up. Then, after a deliberately dramatic pause, created by a carefully calculated hiatus in the chimney-smoke, the winner of the Grand Prize was declared.

Thus it was only after the announcement that the faithful fell into extreme states. Supporters of the winner would begin delightedly cheering, jumping about, embracing, and waving placards with the author's portrait, or an enlargement of the book's dust-jacket, just like in a football stadium after a goal. Meanwhile, all those disappointed—by definition far more numerous—would sink into embittered melancholy and despair. Some among them would take it as a deep personal tragedy. Unable to live down this defeat, they either rushed belligerently at the winner's joyful acolytes, resulting sometimes in pitched battles, or, in a state of deep mental torment, took that step from which there is no return—usually by means of self-immolation. For this purpose they had cans of gasoline and matchboxes conveniently to hand, presciently acquired well in advance.

Because of the great press of people in the vicinity, this act was potentially catastrophic not only for themselves—an extremity to some degree understandable, even justified—but also for the circle of innocent bystanders who took a less apocalyptic view of a sporting defeat. For this reason, after a series of major disasters had been avoided by a hair's-breadth, the authorities finally realized that something must be done.

A special taskforce, known as the "Crisis Management Headquarters," was set up. It included psychologists, sociologists, anthropologists, theologians, philologists, pathologists, cynologists and astrologers, as well as publishers' representatives, who were also a legitimately interested party. To everyone's surprise, a quick and easy solution was achieved—which only goes to show that the tangle of human affairs can always be sorted out with reason and goodwill, especially if a practical remedy is available. In this case, the answer was simplicity itself: just increase the number of awards!

The Grand Prize remained, for all publishers, an obsessive object of desire, but the frenzy surrounding it subsided to some degree when other, newer awards began to spring up like mushrooms after rain. The operational side was taken over by the publishers, as men of the trade, and this made perfect sense. All the technicalities attendant on the founding of new awards were handled by them: naming, determining of criteria and conditions for entry, choice of jury, finding of sponsors, and even the occasional establishing of endowments.

As the whole thing gained momentum, it became obvious that the one element crucial to the reputation of an award was its name. Other factors mattered too, of course, but even a richly endowed award might sink into obscurity purely because of a poorly chosen title. *Nomen est omen*.

Such was, for instance, the fate of the first award set up after the Grand Prize. Its founder thought, for some reason, that the most appropriate name would be: the Lesser Prize. This prize, however, was never even awarded, for the simple reason that no-one entered for it, even though the desperate organizers, as a last resort, guaranteed all competitors an attractive gift, ranging from a year's subscription to the *Hunting Club Bulletin*, to a box season ticket at a puppet theatre, to a daring speleological expedition for two, inclusive of an unlimited supply of lamp-carbide.

Among the other awards which met a similar fate, the most outstanding examples included the Lewd Rooster (awarded to the most outstanding collection of recipes for aphrodisiac chicken hors-d'oeuvres), the Jolly Funeral (for the most upbeat catalogue of spring-time funeral accessories), the Hollow Drum Award (for the best anthology of original hollow-log tom-tom poetry) and the Prickly Flowerpot (awarded to the best-illustrated book on patio-and-windowbox giant cactus-rearing).

After these and a few other devastating experiences, it was finally realized that an award's best chance of success was to be named after some dead great author. The greater the stature of the author, the higher the reputation the award would have. Unfortunately, this plan too was not without difficulties. Even in the richest of national literatures, the number of great writers wasn't nearly sufficient to meet the needs of the far more numerous publishers all wanting to be the founder of some award.

Rescue from this predicament was first sought in a somewhat less rigorous interpretation of the term "stature." What does it mean, after all—a writer of great "stature"? Who is supposed to decide? Literature professors? They are notoriously at odds in their opinions, they can hardly wait for the next opportunity to bicker rancorously about something—seldom discreetly but always in public. Besides, they are chronically underpaid.

Once the publishers got the hang of that scenario, a great burden was lifted from their hearts. Experience revealed that it is not at all difficult to find an academic literary critic who will, if you just ask him nicely, affirm with the full weight of his learning and the authority of his tenured Chair, that any name in the history of literature is of significant stature, even though other academic types dismiss it as being second-rate or even quite insignificant. An appropriate diploma or writ of confirmation could be supplied to this end—constituting something like a certificate of lasting merit, and differing in hardly any respect from the sort of ceremonial scroll used to grant lifetime tenure of a professorship.

This led to a considerable increase in the number of literary luminaries available to add luster to newly founded awards. Now any entry in a directory of writers or a Who's Who granted eligibility, even the merest mention consisting of a bare couple of lines. The only remaining condition was that the author in question be already dead. But even this opening up of the award-naming field could not satisfy the publishers' burgeoning appetites: they had now realized that there was no need for them to restrict themselves to organizing just one award apiece. Far from it—the ideal solution, for them, would be to confer as many awards as they published titles, so that not one book need go undeservedly ignored.

And so, inexorably, the tide of events swept away the last taboo. Once the least distinguished of all the deceased authors was used up, there was no recourse but to conscript the names of the living; a certificate of stature having been obtained for each. Without the certificate no name was worth its salt. The sanctioning of this ultimate permissiveness provoked a number of caustic and unfriendly comments, but the publishers didn't blench; and in due course, the dust settled.

Public opinion stirred mildly only one last time, when some of the awards began to be issued to their own namesakes; but any social innovation is likely to be frowned upon at first. Once people got used to it, and accepted the novelty as part of the natural order, no-one paid that much attention to it, unless some really outrageous liberty were taken. After all, it was a bit on the excessive side for an author to win, not once but eight times in a row, the award bearing his own name, but each time the jury categorically assured the public that they were guided solely by artistic criteria, so no-one was able to find fault with their decision.

This problem resolved, publishers could breathe a collective sigh of relief. They now had control of all the true determining factors regarding book sales, and quite understandably, being businessmen, that was their chief concern. They had the power to make the work appear in a volume of suitably portentous size, with an irresistible cover (its contents teasingly hinted at on the flaps thereof), with quotes and blurbs on the back seeming to recommend the work mightily, with a conspicuous claim that it was at least the third edition, with another conspicuous claim that the author was already a bestseller, and to top it all off, a banderole announcing, in florid letters, that the book had received a major literary prize.

All this apart, nothing else was required than to expose the manuscript to the editorial procedure, which, in terms of medical analogy, was the moment of conception, because the birth of a book follows a series of stages traceable to that one moment. The intervening period, in many ways, resembled pregnancy: nausea and vomiting were typical of the early stages, and the average duration was—until the invention of computers—about nine months.

There was, however, one important difference. While humans need a midwife only at the moment of birth, books demand comparable assistance throughout the entire pregnancy. A single midwife, moreover, is not enough. For a book to be born, a whole team of midwives is required, each with their own responsibility: editor, copy-editor, technical editor, typist, proofreader, printer, binder. Unfortunately, it's long been well known what happens to children who have too many midwives.

When an editor receives a manuscript, nausea, or feelings of seasickness normally associated with pregnancy, grip him for obvious reasons. Opening the cardboard folder—the first to do so, after the author himself—the editor reads the first few paragraphs, a page at most, and that is enough to send him rushing, hand clamped to his mouth, eyes bulging, towards the men's room. Along the way he might stumble, trip over various obstacles, and not infrequently arrive at his destination on all fours. There he lingers for a protracted spell, head bent low over the toilet bowl, and when he returns finally, pale and drawn, to his desk, the first thing he does is to push the folder aside or hide it in a drawer so he needn't look at it, lest the very sight induce a fresh wave of sickness.

A while later, having to some degree composed himself, he makes an attempt that, from experience, he knows will not succeed; yet, driven by desperation, he feels compelled to try. Humbly, timidly, he taps on the director's door, to propose the ultimate heresy: abortion. His justification for this is more than reasonable. The fetus is incurably, genetically flawed. Would it not be better, then, to terminate this pregnancy before it is too late?

Mere moments after stepping into the office with this suggestion, the unfortunate editor comes flying out of it head first, propelled by a torrent of rebukes and recriminations, and more often than not followed by some object, usually large, hard and angular, that happens to be within the director's easy reach. How could he entertain so brutal an idea as abortion? What were these flaws he was talking about? Would the book be born coverless, or without pages, perhaps? With its cover crumpled and torn? Or maybe the binding was destined to come unstitched? Of course not! So, what flaws?

Oh, it was mental, was it? Aha! Learning difficulties? Retarded? Suffering from Down's Syndrome, perhaps? So what? Why should a book be clever, if she looks good? Looks sell books, not wit or spirituality. Can you see wit or spirituality at first glance? No. Can they catch the buyer's eye? Of course they can't. So! There! "Besides," says the director, concluding his tirade, immediately before grabbing an ashtray or a paperweight to hurl, in righteous fury, after the retreating editor, "if it really matters to you whether the book is stupid, roll up your sleeves and spiritualize it to your heart's content. That way at least you'll do something towards earning the salary you get, which is way too high!"

The crestfallen editor then returns to his desk, pulls the folder out of the drawer (or wherever he has hidden it) and somehow suppresses the disgust rising within him. He stares dully at the thing while every shade of despair drifts across his face. Then, darkly contemplating his narrowed options, he does what all pregnant women do: begins stuffing himself. Not with food, as they do; but with drink. The motivation, however, is the same.

Having satisfied his urge, he comes to a decision. If his youthful energy has not entirely withered away (which happens pretty early in this profession) he will tackle the job, though it be as arduous as a miner's. But unlike miners, who at least have the option of taking early retirement, not to mention the gratitude of those who think of them while warming themselves over a stove in winter, he faces a full forty years of godawful toil—with the absolute certainty that all his labors will go forever unsung. Who, indeed, except his closest relatives, pays any attention to the editor's name, printed in the smallest visible type on the publisher's imprint page? And even if someone were to notice, how could they possibly begin to guess at the vast effort exerted by the editor in order to bring to minimal decency something that, by its very nature, was incapable of being made decent?

Rewriting will be the first line of attack. The editor will work sentence by sentence, eliminating the gratuitous, re-ordering what is left, patching holes and making countless other corrections, changes and improvements—all in the grim struggle to instill some spark of meaning into a thing that, as originally presented, possessed none. No-one knows better than editors how rare is the gift of basic literacy—let alone fine style—among those with literary ambitions. Any illusions he might have held on that subject are rapidly dispelled.

As a rule, the climax comes in the fourth hour of labor. On the editor's desk there repose the same number of pages: four—all so scribbled over with transpositions and deletions that no typesetter would agree to set them, however desperate he or she might be for work. The problem is finding someone willing to retype the text. This individual will require many virtues—kindliness, patience, self-abnegation, keen insight, sharp eyesight and above all, nerves of steel—a set of qualities rarely found all at once among the practitioners of that ill-paid craft.

It dawns on the editor, inevitably, that at this rate he will never make the director's deadline. To compose and fortify himself a little, he will take another good swig or two from the bottle he keeps to hand, to render first aid on precisely such occasions. Then, his spirits raised somewhat, he will devise an ingenious strategy: to give up on the corrections and write, all by himself, a whole new text. Its inspiration will come from the stammering original, but nothing more. This will save him the trouble of retyping, and there may well be collateral advantages.

So the guy rolls up his sleeves, elevates his spirits a little more (this is mandatory), skims rapidly on to the end of the manuscript, catching some vague sense thereby of what the author was straining to say, and sets out to render his own take on the same topic. It will, of course, be devoid of any high artistic pretensions, but at least it will be innocent of complete absurdities—also of truisms masquerading as profundities; empty verbiage, lacking even the truth of truisms; and internal inconsistencies (to dispel inconsistencies with logic, experience and common sense is beyond his remit). Each sentence will now have a subject and—at least implicitly—a predicate, representing a major improvement on the original text.

This almost-creative writing will remain forever eclipsed. The director will never notice it because he will be even less willing to read the finished book than he was to read the manuscript. His basic perception of himself is as a talented paper-merchant. He buys paper cheaply, imprints it with some sort of pattern of letter-motifs (it doesn't matter which, they're all the same to him, he doesn't distinguish one from another), then he resells it, but at a much higher price. Nothing could be simpler. He really can't fathom why some people throw away good money on those patterns, but he is most certainly grateful that they do. How else would he make his moolah, if it weren't for their eccentric habit?

It goes hard with the editor, to be overlooked like this. All very well, he didn't expect a raise, although a raise would undoubtedly be justified, but he might at least have been congratulated. As it is, not having received so much as a perfunctory "Thank you," his first enthusiasm quickly fades. If he is genuinely conscientious, he will subject two or three more manuscripts to the same treatment, after which, despite increasingly frequent and larger doses of liquid inspiration, the unmitigated pointlessness of his efforts will overwhelm him. Why bust a gut, when at the end of the day it makes not a blind bit of difference whether he succeeds or fails? In future, instead of breaking his head over rewrites and improvements, he will reduce his role as midwife to two mature and necessary acts: composing the imprint, which will occupy one whole page, and passing the manuscript on to the copy-editor, who will process it further.

The copy-editor's job allows no evasions, no short-cuts—the manuscript must be read right through, word for word. Diagonal and other such techniques will be of no use here, despite the fact that the end result may suggest that he used no other method. But thorough as it must be, and usually is, the copy-editor's reading is of a peculiar kind: the meaning of the text is entirely lost on him. His sole brief is to detect and eliminate orthographical and grammatical errors.

A sentence may be utterly devoid of meaning, but if the spelling and grammar are correct, not forgetting the tense-sequences, verbal declensions and (this being the copy-editor's chief anxiety) if all the commas are properly positioned, then so far as he is concerned, the manuscript in question has achieved perfection. No doubt about it.

Like an over-assiduous linguistic policeman, his sole *raison d'etre* is to apply the rules; nothing else is of interest. What should he care about some meaning or other, when it has no stated parameters, and therefore falls outside his jurisdiction? Meanings and suchlike are civilian matters. Someone else, supposedly, will look after the meaning. Supposedly. In their zeal, copy-editors often go too far; nevertheless, they stick to the general principle: better to mow down ten innocents than let one criminal escape.

The typesetters' reading is even more specialized. Although not forbidden by absolute decree, it is established by long tradition that typesetters should forego any sort of comprehension of the text. They make the fewest mistakes when typing a document in some foreign language of which they haven't the slightest grasp. The more alien the language, the less they understand of it, the better. If they do not know a single word of it, the probability is they will not make a single mistake. On the other hand, the better they know the language the more errors they commit. And most of all, of course, in their mother tongue.

Regrettably, it isn't possible only to give them foreign texts to work on. The majority of the work they receive is actually in their mother tongue. This gave rise to a serious conundrum: how to confound their attempts, voluntary or otherwise, to understand what they're typing? Numerous strategies were devised to this end. The first to be invented were typically crude and human. Right in your face, as it were.

Applicants for typesetting jobs were put through intelligence tests. Only those whose score didn't exceed the level of imbecility were hired. Bovine, native stupidity was prized above all. A candidate required just enough intellect to distinguish individual letters and punctuation marks; anything beyond that was dismissed as excessive.

This discriminatory practice, which violated democracy's fundamental principle of equality for all citizens regardless of I.Q. and natural hair color, had to be abandoned finally after a scandal that erupted when a printing-house of dubious reputation briefly hired specially trained monkeys as typesetters. They offered in their defense the plea that this was the only foolproof means of obviating every vestige of comprehension, and so of eliminating all typing errors.

The first voice raised in protest against this brazen abuse of animals was the Forest Primate Preservation Committee, part of the Society for the Protection of Anthropoids. Committee members ardently rebutted any claim that their protégées could not understand the texts in question. Quite the contrary, they said: any macaque, when trained to type, can also understand what he is typing, even if he doesn't indicate as much by any outward sign. And that, precisely, is the source of potential danger to these benign and intelligent creatures: nothing is likely to corrupt their primeval tranquility so much as a foray into the trackless morasses of the human screed.

After an inevitable delay, the typesetters' union voiced its protest too. They were just as implacably opposed to macaque labor in the printing-houses, but for entirely different reasons. For them, monkeys represented the most blatant example of unfair competition. Monkeys agreed to work overtime for a far smaller wage (three and a half bananas a day came to be the norm). Health insurance was much cheaper for them, partly because veterinary treatment is generally less expensive than its human counterpart, and also because macaques are rarely ill. They didn't need hot lunches, or monthly travel cards; they didn't need vacations because they never got tired; and they had no concept of a trade union, and thus no concept of a strike.

Denied the right to engage morons and monkeys, the printing-houses had no recourse but to invent some other way of distracting their able-minded typesetters from their premeditated, mischievous concentration on the meaning of the texts they were typing. Here the employers had to act furtively, because of the typesetters' fierce opposition to any interference in this regard: they were jealous of their hard-won privilege, to gain full insight into the literature before their eyes, even at the cost of a much higher rate of error.

First clandestine hypnosis was attempted, both individually and *en masse*, but the results of this were wholly unforeseen: typesetters really did make fewer typos, but, as a by-product of their enhanced mental focus, they began inserting into the text various interpolations of their own. Though mainly in the form of parentheses, footnotes, endnotes, afterwords and addenda, these were often lengthy and seldom flattering to the authors. Moreover, they were frequently expressed in language quite alien to the usual norms of academic pedantry; in this way some rather peculiar, and deeply unwelcome, critical editions were produced.

After this, certain bio-active substances, known as "mickeys," were slipped into the food and drink served in the printing-house canteen, intended to induce a mild stupor and so discourage careful reading. But this, too, had to be abandoned, because it was impossible to ensure that only the typesetters would be affected. It was of no advantage whatsoever to have the entire staff draped around the office in a narcotic haze, displaying a total disinclination towards work, just to keep the typesetters in that condition.

All else having failed, the management were forced

to resort to the ultimate and, if past experience is anything to go by, most reliable means of settling any issue
involving humans—bribery. The printing-house owners
calculated that the cheapest solution would be to offer
special bonuses and sweeteners to those typesetters who
overlooked the meaning of the text they were working
on. This being tricky to police, at first they just asked
for a signed affidavit. This was a specially made-up form,
just a single sheet, by which the typesetter affirmed, on
his word of honor, that he hadn't the slightest idea what,
if anything, the work might be about.

These statements proliferated out of control, and
before long not a single typeset appeared without an
accompanying guarantee of incomprehension, seriously threatening to drain all the resources put aside for
the purpose. The bosses were forced to concede that
honor is not, after all, the most universal of human
qualities. Some other indirect monitoring system, even
a less honorable one, had to be found in order to render
the true state of affairs unambiguous.

After devoting some thought to the problem, the
bosses reached a solution as simple and straightforward as Columbus's Egg. Typos! The more there were,
the more likely the typesetter was to have taken in the
meaning of the manuscript. To punish this attempt
at comprehension, rather than the mistakes *per se*, the
typesetter's salary would now be savagely docked that
month, rather than increased.

This was unfair only to those honest typesetters who
genuinely failed to follow the text but made mistakes
anyway owing to poor eyesight, imperfect skill, mental
distress arising from domestic or romantic crises, alco-
holism or other, equally innocuous causes. The bosses,
however, suffered no pangs of conscience on that account. You can't be fair to everyone; there's no such
creature as immaculate justice.

Excessive typing errors, caused mainly by the type-

setters' struggle for the basic human right to understand a text, completely denied that same right to the
last midwives in the line who read the manuscript before its actual printing—the proofreaders. That's the
way it is in a democracy. Like justice, democracy is never perfect. Someone has to be the underdog.

In fact, it's impossible to pick up on some putative
meaning when you're devoting every ounce of your attention to the hunt for variants from the original. Big
mistakes are no problem, they're easily spotted, they
stick out like sore thumbs. It's the little nits that cause
the mischief, the ones which are hardest to nail. Those
are the proofreaders' nightmare. It isn't such a problem
when they quite plainly make no sense at all, when, for
instance, there's a letter positioned where it absolutely
can't be, making a word into gobbledygook and thus
obvious.

On the other hand, a letter might be wrong and yet
fit in nicely, creating another word, so that the meaning turns into something the author never intended,
if he intended anything at all; producing in effect a
false meaning. So how are you meant to find it? In your
efforts to spot typos, you can't follow the meaning, so
you can't see that the meaning is out of synch. The
typesetter clunks out, for example, "blight" instead of
"light." Both are plausible words in many contexts, but
which was it actually supposed to be? Try as you might,
you are a long way from enlightenment. It's worse still
when he types "not" for "now," or vice versa.

Of course, that typo may not make much difference
to one sentence in a work of fiction, most readers will
never notice that anything is amiss. Even if they do,
they won't waste time over it; who has time for such
trivialities? In fact, it isn't the only typo in the book.
Sadly, there are some inveterate pedants, idle lay-
abouts with nothing better to do than make a note of
the spelling mistakes in the latest novel. They have no

compunction about ruining their own copy, for which they paid good money, and sending it by parcel post to the director of the publishing house, along with a cover letter phrased in the most scathing language. They demand their money back, threaten to write to the newspapers, even mention the possibility of litigation.

The director couldn't care less about blight or light, but he has to maintain the reputation of the house, which is no trifling matter; so he summons the unfortunate proofreader for a dressing-down. The guilty proofreader has to stand to attention, bolt upright like a soldier reporting to the commandant. The director, using numerous high-faluting words and implicit threats, hauls him over the coals. First the poor fellow is told that, while his job is essentially parasitic and unnecessary, it may not, even so, be carried out in a spirit of irresponsible sloppiness. What kind of a dog's breakfast was this? Was he aware that publishing is a province of the elevated realm of Culture and—it may be asserted—Art? If anything of this kind should happen again, the proofreader would have to look for alternative employment, but not in publishing; in that field, all doors would be forever closed to him.

The wretch retreats from the office, bowing and scraping. Next the director orders his secretary to send five fresh copies of the book in question to the citizen who complained, as compensation; and to recover the cost of this operation (each book charged at full recommended retail price, without reductions) from the proofreader's salary. Excellent! That'll knock a bit of sense into him. The matter is resolved, not only by a salutary lesson, but also by means of good business sense: five more copies rung up in the sales ledger—in a somewhat devious way, but what does that matter?

Galleys arrive once more from the typesetters' workrooms: crude paper pages no wider, but several times longer, than a regular page. The proofreader reads them again, this time with even less chance to engage more deeply with the meaning of the text. Fixated on the search for typographical errors, he spreads the manuscript before him, spelling every word out letter by letter. His eyes water with effort, lines of text waver and swim before them, and when he alights on any kind of aberration, particularly of the devious sort, the conviction grows within him that some mischief is afoot. All these mistakes cannot be accidental, some of them strike him as deliberate distortions, acts of sabotage in fact—often rude, or even downright obscene.

A hockey puck printed with an initial "f," how to explain that mistake? Or the omission of the first "g" from the distinguished Latin tag, *Cogito, ergo sum?* Here it should all be correct because Latin is the most foreign of foreign languages to the typesetter. It cannot, by definition, be his mother tongue. Then there is art, a noble concept indeed, forever accruing an extra, opening "f."

Proofreaders might, one supposes, compensate for their huge frustrations in the workplace by reading those same books later, once they have appeared. It should be easy enough, now that the book is available, finished and complete, just to pick it up and read it, to probe its deepest meaning to their heart's content, now as a common reader, no longer as a nervous error-seeker.

But it will never happen. It would violate the profession's ultimate taboo. Not for love or money will a proofreader re-open a book he has once corrected—primarily because the very sight of it revives the terrible stress and trauma he had to endure while he was working on it. Then there is his never-extinguished anxiety that the job was not properly done, that some mistakes slipped through, perhaps even a few major ones, horribly perverting the meaning.

The fear of such discoveries, now it is too late to do

anything about them, overwhelms any curiosity. Better to live in blissful ignorance, believing all is well, than to suffer the shock of uncovering monstrous howlers. And all this, ultimately, on account of those good-for-nothing grumblers who for reasons of sheer small-minded malice keep burrowing through the text in search of typographical errors and then, sneaks and snitches that they are, go writing letters of complaint to the director and spoil his mood as well. And all for the sake of squeezing out a few miserable freebies in the form of some books they'll then sell off cheap! If it weren't for them, the proofreaders' lot might be endurable, jogging along nicely until early retirement, obtained perhaps on the plea of job-related invalidity. And after retirement it would be plain sailing.

In all this, probably the least of their worries is the fact that, to all intents and purposes, they've read not a single one of the manuscripts that have passed through their hands in the course of their whole career. But why would only the proofreaders be bothered by this? They're hardly the odd ones out. None of the other midwives who help bring books into the world are any keener readers. Neither are any of them expected to be. Whether they read them or not, books will be born willy-nilly. It's an immutable law of the universe. Why, after all, usurp the right of those poor souls who are prepared to do it of their own free will, without coercion, and even in their boundless naiveté pay for the privilege: that is to say, the readers?

While on the face of it everyone's happy and everything's hunky-dory, one person remains in constant anxiety, try as he might not to show it: the publishing-house director. He can't rid himself of the suspicion that the company is full of redundant hangers-on. Do they really need so many midwives to bring just one single book into the world? He wouldn't mind there being such a lot of them if they volunteered their services, but unfortunately he has to pay them each month to do jobs which strike him as entirely unnecessary—and therefore pretty expensive at any price.

The accountant comes forward to submit the payroll, nervous and hesitant, wearing a hard hat just to be on the safe side, and all the director's blood rushes to his face. His heart starts to pound, cold sweat breaks out all over his body, he grinds his teeth, sometimes he growls and begins frothing at the mouth. So far as he is concerned, this business is tantamount to armed robbery. To sign his authorization on the total sum, on a figure that leaves him gasping and choking, his eyes bulging out of his head, seems no different to him from being forced to surrender his wallet to a highwayman at gunpoint.

Left to himself after this brief encounter, the director, quite understandably, sinks into a deeply depressed, even catatonic state. Even a few prolonged autistic episodes have been known to occur. Everything suddenly seems to him gloomy, hopeless and meaningless. After a while the stress eases a bit and he attempts, perhaps involuntarily, to find some relief in simple daydreaming: a natural defensive reaction post-trauma.

In his imagination, a far more fairly organized publishing world takes shape, one in which there are no unnecessary middlemen between author and printing-house. No editor, no copy-editor, no graphics and technical editors, no typesetter, no proofreader. All these wastrels disappear as if rubbed out with an eraser, the manuscript passes from the writer's hands directly to the printing-house, and most important of all, the total at the bottom of the weekly payroll transforms itself into something much more reasonable.

It's a rude awakening, to return from this rose-tinted vision to hard reality. No wonder so many directors seek solace of some kind, usually out of a bottle, though others resort to more sleazy consolations. Who can blame them? Life is no picnic for managing directors; the essence of their being is under threat. (Well, their financial status, actually, but that may well be the essence of their essence.)

And then, quite out of the blue, when it was least expected, a unique opportunity arose for this vision to become reality. The general advancement of mankind in all respects, and particularly in the field of technology, brought forth a device, quite compact, but powerful enough to enable even the boldest dreams of a publishing-house director to come true.

The computer!

In no other field, probably, has the computer brought about such a revolution as in publishing. Preparation of manuscripts for printing now became incomparably cheaper, easier, faster—what could be more gratifying to a director? All the same, the process was gradual. It started when authors began bringing their texts into the office on diskettes, rather than in cardboard folders full of typewritten sheets of paper. This very first step was sufficient to do away straight off with two of the many midwives who had for so long fiddle-faddled about in publishing: the typesetters and the proofreaders.

Nobody needed their services any longer, because there was no type to set and no proofs to read. An unequivocal saving, since the writers didn't demand any increase in payment for submitting their work on diskette. Quite the contrary: the computer was a huge boon to them as well, especially once they'd actually learned to use it. This process was hardly straightforward; sometimes it was accompanied by headaches and foul tempers; but we won't go into that here, the subject having been covered at length in other quarters. No story benefits from repetition, even if the topic seems inexhaustible.

As computer programs gradually improved and as

authors, not without a degree of pride and self-congrat-
ulation, became more and more adept at using them
(or so they thought), scope was found for further ra-
tionalization in the publishing business. Thrifty directors made no attempt to conceal their delight at this. It
seemed that not only were authors able to submit raw
text on diskette to the editorial office, to be taken up by
the editor and then the proofreader, finally to be passed
on to the technical editor for graphic design. No, now
they brought the print-ready copy. The work of the entire publishing and printing-house departments was
now completed in the author's home, whence emerged
a delightful finished product: namely, "tracing papers."

No technical editor's meddling was needed any
more. His job was done quite satisfactorily by the author
himself. What was there to agonize about? It's easy as
pie: you let the text "break" itself up into pages, which
really isn't difficult, a few strokes on the keyboard will
do the trick; you don't even need to use the mouse.
Then you do the graphic layout, a little at a time: titles,
defining subtitles, spaces between letters and lines, in-
dentations, margins, tabulation of paragraphs, and so
on. It's all very straightforward once you get the hang
of it, and tends to be repetitive, though with footnotes
and equations (which are also of feminine gender in
many languages) there may be occasional problems.
They may act rather capriciously, as females are wont
to do, but such difficulties can be got over one way or
another. If the worst comes to the worst, the author can
simply remove them from the manuscript, a decision
nobody else could take from a position of better authority—and good riddance. Footnotes and formulae
just get in the way of reading.

Finally, all that remained for the author to do was
to print the prepared pages onto semi-transparent,
greasy-looking "tracing paper" with his laser printer.
This kind of paper is a bit of a nuisance, admittedly;

it tends to wrinkle and crumple, but it is considerably cheaper than film; some hardships have to be borne in the pursuit of such huge benefits. The actual print-out is a mirror image of what the readers will see, with the words running from right to left. This procedure has not yet been fully perfected; it retains a certain degree of tetchiness and unpredictability, but given care, the monster will be tamed. With just a little effort the results will be beautiful. The text never sees any editorial offices, no typesetting or proofreading are required—the work goes from the author's hands straight to the printing press. No delays, no lost or wasted time. It's a new era!

The director is in seventh heaven, having just fired, as "technologically redundant," the editor, the technical editor and the copy-editor. Now that authors submit works completely print-ready, there's clearly nothing for these surplus personnel to do. Not inconceivably, some editorial work might still be of benefit, but scribbling on the tracing paper is out of the question. How would that look? It will surely brook no alterations, now that everything is finished!

So thanks to computers, everything turned rosy in the garden almost overnight. The whole publishing process was streamlined and made respectable, much as people strive to do when organizing their own reproductive life. It was also intensely patriarchal. No evasions, no chopping and changing, no flights of individuality. And definitely no immorality. Basic order had to be maintained. In short, an entirely new set of protocols.

First comes the marriage facilitator, also known as the matchmaker or literary agent, to the girl's father, alias the publishing house director. The matchmaker praises the groom, i.e. the writer, and if the groom is accepted—which may crucially depend on whether he has the tracing papers ready, since everything else is more or less insignificant—a wedding is arranged immediately, there being no grounds for holding long engagements. Admittedly, it is not entirely clear who the bride might be in this analogy, but that isn't very important, as no-one canvasses her opinion. She is an obedient family member, in all things respectful of her father's wishes.

One official, the registrar, has no analogue but even without his presence, a contract is signed; purely because of legal terminology, it is called an author's, not a marriage contract. The offices of a priest may be provided to grace this glad and festive occasion, if a participant specifically requests it and furnishes his fee. Whether because this last condition is rarely met, or for some other reason, the priest is generally absent, although he would perfectly complement the idyllic picture.

The groom receives the dowry (i.e. the advance), and hopes in his naiveté that his father-in-law will continue to provide plentiful support in the form of honoraria. A special clause in the contract explains this at length; monthly payments may even be stipulated, but this remains largely a hollow promise; the bride's father has no intention whatever of throwing good money after bad. He's of the fixed opinion that the advance was already over-generous—for a daughter like this *he*, not the groom, should have received a dowry! The groom should consider himself extremely fortunate to have been accepted, destitute as he is, into this respectable house, instead of pestering people with his fads and fancies.

The only person to come off well out of it all is the matchmaker. Ten percent of the dowry goes to him, and to make sure the groom doesn't forget to pay up, which he is obliged to do but which might slip his mind in the midst of all the jubilation, the matchmaker makes use of the simple expedient of handling the entire transaction personally, merely retaining his ten percent cut, in other words, his commission. Happy bank-book, happy hearts.

After the wedding, the newlyweds naturally retire to the privacy of the marital bedroom. Were they human beings, a tactful and circumspect narrator would only follow them to the door of this hallowed chamber and no further. He would not dream of peeking inside, not even through the keyhole, although it is entirely possible that this would disappoint the secret hopes of some of his more lecherous readers. The most that such prurient individuals can hope for is some tasteful euphemism, or perhaps a skillful rendition of the sort of creaking and panting noises one might hear if one actually pressed one's ear to the door. If this is not enough for them, such sensualists have no option but to stop reading decent prose altogether. It isn't their thing. Let them slake their lusts over outright pornography.

But if it's publishing that's going on in there, the narrator's position is much more comfortable. In these bridal chambers nothing takes place that would be unfit for description in the most explicit terms: a no-holds-barred account, without being coy, since there's no danger of upsetting even those most sensitive souls who blush crimson at the first most innocuous reference to romance, and are capable of fainting dead away at the merest hint of the erotic! On the contrary. Not even a whisper of amorousness, which anyone, surely, no matter how prudish they are, might expect to encounter on a wedding night, is in evidence here. It's all banal, bureaucratic, drearily prosaic.

In strides the author, into the office of the director's secretary—excited, all a-tremble, as befits this unique moment. Since the computer revolution, she alone has retained her position in the editorial offices. For a while the director considered firing her too, much like

Ebenezer Scrooge, such was his redundancy-induced euphoria. But on regaining his former sanity to some extent, he realized he couldn't do everything by himself. What would the world say if a director had no secretary, and was obliged to take all his own telephone calls? Not to mention making his own coffee.

On the other hand, overpaying her for these few menial duties would be just as unseemly. Had he not just relieved himself of the burden of signing those accursed payrolls for all those unnecessary editorial staff? Why should he take more of the same punishment? Then, like a revelation, the answer struck him. He would combine beauty with utility. This secretary would have something to do in between answering phone calls, opening envelopes and washing coffee cups; something other than sitting idly gazing into space, reading the newspaper, solving crosswords, filing her nails (which, for some reason, particularly unnerved him) and generally lolling about. (Whenever he caught her in any of these poses, he would feel himself come one step closer to a heart attack.)

The solution required a certain financial investment, but that, alas, was unavoidable. To make an omelet you have to crack a few eggs. For a start, he bought her a new computer. Second-hand, but still in good condition. Fully adequate for her needs. Why, after all, waste money on state-of-the-art hardware, when everything to do with computers becomes obsolete in a few months? Those electronics geeks were forever improving things, tweaking this and that. Then he sent her on a one-month accelerated course in computer literacy. There was a two-month course as well, but that cost more, and besides, the classes took place not only in the evening but during working hours, and that wouldn't do at all. Why should he pay for her to take time off as well?

In any case, she didn't need to become a professional programmer, she only needed to learn basic editorial skills; the ones that, along with the author's tracing papers, put the finishing touches to the pre-printing process. A few bits and pieces, really. Conceivably the writer could have provided them too, and so achieved maximum speed and economy, but progress, unfortunately, has yet to go so far. What she had to do was compose the so-called zero-sheet pages, those at the start and end of the novel, and make films for the covers. Nothing much. She just needed to master a few patterns; then it was plain sailing. Just type in the few dozen words required, and choose an illustration—and that was it. No great expertise was required. A common secretary would be quite up to the job.

And so, into the office of the director's secretary strides the author, excited and all the rest of it, and she comes straight to the point, without beating about the bush and sometimes without a word of a hello. Her whole demeanor makes it clear that she—just like her employer—holds authors in the deepest possible contempt. Without them, her life would be so much easier! If nothing else, she wouldn't have had to struggle with that mind-numbing computer course, which she barely managed to scrape through; and she'd have so much less to do.

Besides, those writer types are always full of stupid questions and keep moaning and whining all the time. They're all so full of themselves, just because they've managed to scribble something. Big deal! How much would their text be worth without her expertise in preparing the covers (not to mention the imprint)? It's the looks that make a book, not the guff inside. The majority of people haven't time for it—she herself being an excellent example. She doesn't care to remember when she last read anything, and can you wonder? Who would ever read a book once they'd got to know a few authors? A person who's never met one might possibly fall for reading. To a reader like that, authors are just disembodied names, abstract, not real people. But just lay eyes on them once, or like her, get an eyeful every day! It would never again cross the reader's mind to go near or touch a book, let alone actually read one. No earthly way!

"Good day," says the author, grinning from ear to ear. He reckons the friendly approach can never do any harm, especially not in this sort of situation. Which may be very true, except that friendliness isn't always met with friendliness, as soon becomes apparent.

The secretary glances up sourly from the outspread fingers of her left hand. She has been deeply preoccupied with her manicure. If there's anything she hates in this world, it's being interrupted in this most sensitive work. She glances a moment at the author's humble figure, then readdresses herself to her long, rounded fingernails, which are conspicuously red—as well they should be! Let's see who's sad enough not to notice them! And the generous sprinkling of silver glitter that gleams so beguilingly as she moves her hands, isn't it just so cool! She's simply in love with herself.

If only this skinny creep had not appeared right now, she could have done her right hand at her leisure. The director will be out of the office all day—a peach of an opportunity. It's such hard work keeping fingernails like hers! It takes her till lunchtime, sometimes even longer. They haven't a clue how intricate it is, how long it can take to get it exactly right.

She starts waving her left hand to and fro to make the nail polish dry faster, then she slowly closes the little bottle and tucks it away in the largest drawer in her desk, which is dedicated solely to her cosmetics. She keeps the drawer permanently locked, the stuff inside is expensive, and you get all sorts of people coming through here. Turn her back once, and she could lose something. Just as well to take a few precautions.

"Gimme!" she says at last.

"Pardon?" says the author, in some confusion. He is still standing in the doorway, clutching under his arm a largish, imitation leather attaché-case, extremely shabby and starting to fall apart.

"Your tracing papers. C'mon, why're you standing there like a bump on a log? I ain't got all day. You brought them with you, yes?"

"Oh, those," says the writer, relieved. "Yes, yes, of course I brought them. Here they are." He hurries up to the secretary's desk and extracts the cardboard folder with the tracing papers from his attaché case. His movements are somewhat nervous and clumsy, which is understandable. This is the first time he has submitted a manuscript for printing. He knows what to expect, he isn't entirely wet behind the ears, yet his excitement and inexperience are telling on him.

He holds out his faded green folder towards the secretary. With its frayed edges, it has clearly seen plenty of use. Some previous owner has written something on the cover in ink, subsequently scored out in ballpoint and covered with a sticky label bearing a new title. The new writing only partially conceals the old.

The look of disgust on the secretary's face is quite plain to see. To take this object in her carefully groomed, hangnail-free hands is the last thing she would do by choice. She indicates, with her eyes only, where the author is to place his folder. And he obeys unhesitatingly.

Then, without a word, the secretary starts up her computer and monitor. What is there to say, after all? Does a surgeon explain to the patient the function of each instrument that will be used in the operation? The silence is broken only by the low hum of the hard-disk drive as the system reboots. Finally, one image remains fixed on-screen.

"Wha's it about?" demands the secretary, in the funereal tone which has become her trademark.

The author would like to repeat his "Pardon?" but something tells him that it would only further infuriate this immaculate lady, so he refrains. Nevertheless, the confusion on his face puts the question for him.

"This," replies the secretary. With the little finger of her right hand she indicates the folder, while carefully keeping it at a safe distance. "Keep it brief, jus' stick to the basics." That warning is given for a very good reason. She knows all too well what authors are like. Enough of their ilk have circulated through here. If you gave them the least encouragement they would start talking about their masterpieces, and once they started there was no stopping them. Blither on and on, they would, to their hearts' content, until you asked yourself why they bothered writing the stuff down when they could give it in recitation just as well. Why, you couldn't help wondering as you listened, did mankind ever abandon the oral tradition for the written one?

"Ah," the author says. He understands. But he doesn't immediately set about summarizing it. First he pauses a little to think it through. What are the "basics"? It cannot be so reduced. Would he have written so much if his work could be boiled down to an abstract? Remove one word, and the book would be destroyed. The book would cave in, collapse upon itself. But there's no point in making that argument just now. This is obviously a very short-tempered woman, with little sympathy for the finer points of literature. A pity; he could, he really could expound the entire narrative to her in detail. In the end she would surely like it. Everyone knows how women love melodramas. Especially if they end in tragedy and pathos. But things being the way they were just now—he would have to keep it brief. The briefer the better.

"Well, you see, it's about this prince from a rotten country, never mind which, there are lots of countries like that, although I can tell you, if you are really interested. . . ."

A lightning-flash from her eyes indicates very clearly the extent of her interest in geography.

"All right, that's not essential, anyway. So, the prince's father dies. . . ."

"It's a fairytale?" the secretary interrupts him.

"Fairytale? No, why?"

"You gotta prince."

"Yes, but not the kind of prince you get in fairytales."

"All right, go on. Just keep it real brief."

"The prince's father did not just die, he was in fact killed."

"Aha, detective novel," the secretary interrupts him again.

"No, no detective, but the father's ghost appears to the prince. . . ."

"So, a horror novel, yeah? About ghosts?" An undertone of imminently snapping patience appears in the secretary's voice.

"No, no, the ghost only appears at the beginning, and then the prince plans his revenge. As it turns out, the king's brother killed the king, to seize his kingdom and also to marry the king's wife, the prince's mother; she's in collusion with the murderer. The murder was particularly heinous—while the king was sleeping, his brother, the prince's uncle, poured into his ear . . ."

"Any sex?" intervenes the secretary, relentless in her efforts to keep down the verbiage.

"Sex?" For a moment the author looks scandalized. "Well, not exactly, although there is a girl who is in love with the prince, but he doesn't care much for her, so in the end she kills herself, even though he benevolently advises her to retire to a nunnery and . . ."

"Awright, awright. I got it. Erotic thriller."

The author opens his mouth to say something. This

generic classification seems somehow incomplete, not quite how he originally conceived it. As his original concept wasn't quite so cut-and-dried, it may be he hasn't retold it very well—he was certainly pressed for time. This was supposed to be a tragedy, a tragedy in the classic tradition. But why argue about it now? Let it be an erotic thriller, if it must. Did it really matter? The crucial thing was that the book be published, regardless of the company it kept; once that was accomplished everything else would tumble into place.

The secretary begins tapping on her keyboard. A window appears on the screen, showing the back cover, the book's spine, and the front cover. At present, all three are blank.

"What title?" she asks, ready to type.

The author scratches his head. "You know, I am in a bit of a dilemma there," he admits reluctantly. "My first intention was for the title to be just the name of this prince, but now it somehow doesn't seem sufficiently . . . how shall I put it? . . . inventive. I might have to give it some more thought, in fact. . . ."

"Well, you writers really aren't easssy to deal with," the secretary hisses at him. Her face is beginning to acquire the shade of the varnish on her left-hand fingernails. "You never have *everything* ready. Always something missing. One guy has no contents page, another forgets about the afterword, another hasn't got the illustrations. And now the title, even! What will we have next? Some day one of you will walk in here without his head! So what do we do now? The book has to go to the printer, it can't hang around while you make up your mind."

The writer gulps, he feels beads of sweat forming all over his body, but not because of the weather. "All right, I mean, it doesn't matter, or not very much, it can be the name of the prince, never mind it not being inventive, I didn't know the circumstances were so urgent. . . ."

"What name! How can you say such a thing? Whoever heard of an erotic thriller without any title, just the name of some stoopid prince? Who in his right mind would ever buy that? Fer chrissakes, do I have to do it all by myself? You people are no use at all."

With a deep sigh, she leans over the keyboard once again. As she types, letters appear immediately on the monitor in the space reserved for the front cover and at the same time vertically along the spine of the book. The name of the author first, and then the title: *The Rotten Ghost of the Monastery*.

Over the secretary's shoulder, the author stares in horrified confusion at the monitor. Her fingers continue to race over the keys. She could go even faster, but she can only type with her right hand, as the polish on the left has not yet dried. With that she saws the air, now near, now far.

Underneath and all around the title, the "illustration" manifests itself. First, the half-naked figure of a buxom beauty, her face contorted with horror, drinking from a small bottle with a skull and crossbones on the label. The author is tempted for a moment to explain that the heroine of this literary work does not drink poison, but drowns herself; but he decides not to mention it. Let sleeping dogs lie. Besides, who cares? Poison or water, it's really no big deal, the important thing is that she kills herself.

The background is soon filled by the massive stone walls of some edifice: a monastery or perhaps a fortress, it's hard to tell. A tall cross stands at the top of one tower, but there are cannons protruding from the battlements. A hybrid, evidently. This building is the headquarters of an order of warrior monks: no other explanation is possible. Wisps of smoke curl from the mouths of two cannons. The writer reflects that this is an anachronism; gunpowder had not yet been invented at the time this work is set, but once more he decides to let it pass. Should he split hairs over such minutiae? And who is going to notice, in any case?

After this, an apparition appears at one of the arrow-slits. The author accepts that this is the ghost, whose presence is now indicated by the title, though the ghost looks more like a vampire. Why would a spirit have two crooked fangs growing out of his upper jaw, and why would a long, thick stake of hawthorn be sticking out of his chest? And he is wearing a black cape, spread wide to expose a lining of crimson silk. Exactly like Dracula. But this, too, passes unopposed. In any case, who really knows what a ghost might look like? In the text, the ghost is described as a big white sheet with two empty slits for eyes, dragging clanking chains behind himself, but that may just be an inaccurate stereotype. Isn't the creativity of the artist, the illustrator, entitled to a dash of poetic license? Which means he shouldn't have to cling to the original text like a drunk to a lamp-post.

The secretary raises her right hand from the keyboard, shifts her chair a little on its castors, regards the covers critically and nods in satisfaction: a job well done. And done quickly, which is far more important. Now to add a final touch of glitter, and she will be able to concentrate on her manicuring once more.

Pulling her chair closer, she takes up the mouse and sets the cursor rapidly but smoothly criss-crossing the screen. The writer observes this as if hypnotized. He can also use a computer, self-taught though he is; he has achieved a certain level of skill and produced the tracing papers himself. Not that it was easy, no, it was a damn tricky business; by the time they were all out of the printer, he was sweating as much as if he had given birth. But he was no match for this secretary. He could never do what she was doing.

In the lower right-hand corner of the front cover, a star-shaped medallion has materialized from nowhere:

golden letters on a silvery background. They're not just eye-catching—they're almost incandescent, leaving violet after-images: "Third edition!" For a passing instant, the author toys with the idea of asking for an explanation—this must be due to some misunderstanding—but he doesn't dare. While he is still wondering how best to handle this situation, another surprise awaits him: in the upper left-hand corner there appears a wide blue band like a silk medal-ribbon, emblazoned with an announcement almost better than the title: "Winner of the Lustful Murder Prize for Best Erotic Thriller of the Year!"

The author coughs raspingly, as if breadcrumbs have caught in his windpipe, and once he has started he can't stop. The secretary proceeds inexorably, paying him no attention. She has long since become inured to this kind of outburst: authors frequently make wheezing-choking sounds behind her back while she works, ill-mannered ingrates that they are. You honor them, you set them up on high, as it were, you pluck them from the hopeless obscurity in which they would have drudged away their lives—but they object, protest, oppose. They don't even express their reservations in a decent manner; rather they resort to these gasps and grating noises. But with luck she will soon be shot of this barbarian. She has only the back cover to throw together, and that will be that.

The five as yet unlacquered fingers resume their quiet drumming on the keyboard, and three shiny declarations emerge on the monitor:

*New masterpiece from a famous author!*
*Irresistible, fascinating, enchanting!*
*Shivers of horror from first line to last!*

And beneath each statement, but in smaller type, is the title of the newspaper or magazine from which the quotation has been snipped. And so it should be. The computer's memory holds more than two hundred such slogans, all at her disposal, ready for instant use. At first she selected them herself, but when she discovered that was unnecessary, she gladly delegated that part of the task to the machine. Why would she bother, in fact, when these contraptions were designed precisely for that purpose? She presses a single key, and the computer automatically selects three overblown pieces of hype. They are chosen at random, but not one has ever been found inappropriate. Quite the reverse. Whatever their order or combination, they always fit the book perfectly.

Finally, the secretary turns back to face the author. He is still coughing, to the point where his eyes have started to bulge; this latest embellishment to the cover has done nothing to help him catch his breath—on the contrary, it seems. She casts him a glance in which contempt and pity struggle for dominance—a look which clearly announces that she has not the slightest intention of offering the poor man a glass of water, let alone a pat on the back. She continues to observe him a few moments longer, now waving her polished nails in front of her face, before saying in a voice of flat, imperiously dismissive authority: "It's done. You can go."

The author obeys at once. What else can he do? Perhaps he should have summoned up some polite valediction, but this cough has really got the better of him, he is still out of control. He's obliged to put a handkerchief over his mouth; tears have sprung to his eyes. He is very embarrassed over this whole coughing incident. What sort of impression will this young lady have of him?

As he steps out of the office he concludes that, all things considered, he has been fortunate. It's true, he had imagined the loss of his publishing virginity in a somewhat more romantic fashion; it's in the nature of literary types to be hopelessly sentimental. But things might have turned out far worse. Had fate, or whoever looks after that sort of thing, destined him to be a male mantis, for instance, which could easily have been the case, you never know what cards you will get dealt, he would now, having finished mating, be deceased— decapitated. Seen from that perspective, does he have anything to complain about? As any schoolboy knows, luck is a very relativistic business.

Let us send the writer on his way. Sooner or later, presumably, he will stop coughing. He has done his duty. A fruitful wedding night lies behind him. Fertilization has been accomplished, a book will soon be brought into the world. But men have never taken much interest in this last aspect of the job.

This is the point at which the manuscript, almost completely prepared, heads for the printing-house. (The secretary has forgotten the prelims sheet, having more urgent, manicure-orientated concerns; it isn't the first time this has happened to her, but she will add it later, although it wouldn't make any difference if those few pages at the front of the novel were completely omitted, no-one ever reads them anyway.) As such, it is the most appropriate point for this narrative voice to leave you, thanking you for your attention.

He, the voice, was hired to describe those moments into which books themselves have no insight—the moments of their creation. He was meant to do so as succinctly as possible, tersely almost, so as not to imperil the narrative dominance of the book's own voice which, in this work, must retain primacy. But it was simply impossible to condense his testimony any further. As you have now had the opportunity to observe, the life of a book is no less thrilling before its birth than after, and therefore deserving of this rather lengthy peroration. . . .

AT LAST!

We were just about starting to think we wouldn't get a word in ever again, in our own *opus*. But that's how it is with humans. You give them an inch and they take a mile. The gentleman appropriates more than half the book for himself, then calls it a "rather lengthy peroration." His penchant for euphemism is quite shameless. But what's done is done. Had we been in a position to hire someone else for the job, someone better inclined toward moderation and restraint, we would have done so with pleasure; but we had no choice. Fortunately for us, he kept to our agreement in one other respect: he avoided most of the vulgarisms that, with humans, always cling to any discussion about the propagation of the species.

So, here we are, at the entrance to an institution for which we books feel the greatest possible repugnance. All that we have said about libraries and bookshops being the scenes of our deepest humiliation is trivial compared with what we have to say about printing-houses. Whoever invented them is for us the Father of Lies, Satan himself! Printing-houses are the real source of all our subsequent sufferings and torments. There it all begins.

When, in very recent times, humans came by the ability to clone themselves—genetics is advancing apace, along with every other branch of science—there was an enormous brouhaha. Everyone and his aunt rose up in protest, hurling abuse at the poor scientists, just because they had made a replica of some miserable sheep. Not that the public gave a fig for that sheep as an individual, people would multiply sheep by the million in any kind of machine, even in a photocopier if they could; the point is that everyone knew that for geneticists sheep are practically the same thing as people, so far as cloning technology is concerned: if a sheep can be cloned, a human can be cloned too.

And that is where the public drew the line: that was something impermissible. Shall the irreplaceable uniqueness of each human individual be endangered by allowing irresponsible geneticists to mass-produce them, as if punching them out, one after another after another? Heaven forbid! Cries of righteous protest against this sacrilege were raised by everyone who cared even in the slightest for man's superior status in the order of things; from liberal priests and intellectual hacks, through lesbian forums and councils for the avocation of sado-masochism, to associations of free fishermen, unions of disabled bus-conductors, even NAMPAT (the universally feared National Association of Milk-delivery Persons and Allied Trades); not to mention gynecologists, obstetricians, midwives and pregnancy advisers, who would all become instantly unemployed. So the geneticists had finally to tuck their tails between their legs and skulk away, abandoning, at least officially, their schemes for people-replication.

An entirely correct attitude, one might say. What ought to be unique must not be mass-produced. True, but why should it apply only to humans? They may be above sheep in some respects, give or take a little; so maybe cloning is acceptable for sheep and not for people. But if the dividing line between sheep and people is intelligence, then all other intelligent species ought to be equally protected.

Books above all, since there is no third intelligent species.

And are we protected from cloning? Is our uniqueness or irreplaceability taken into account? Not in the least! Quite the opposite! For five hundred years people have been madly and frantically multiplying and mass-producing us—and in a totally unregulated fashion which offers us no protection. They have even made of it a respectable trade, one with minor artistic pretensions—the printing trade. It could be claimed, in fact, that humans arrived at the idea of cloning through their experience in this obnoxious context.

In our case, they paid no heed to ethical or humanitarian considerations. Our lot was even worse than that of the poor sheep. At least their fate stirred the Society for the Protection of Animals to protest, however ineffectively, while precisely nobody at all stood up for us. They might have, failing all else, averted their eyes; that we could have understood. But no, instead they extolled the supposed blessings of the printing press. Books would be available to all at last, not only to the privileged elite. Culture and all its attendant civilized values would gain thereby a firm democratic stronghold. No-one, of course, asked us for our opinion. Keep quiet, you! Roll yourselves under the press! And from under that printing press we keep spewing forth, in countless identical copies, all for the benefit of democracy. It's easy enough to plough the juggernaut of democracy over the prostrate back of somebody else.

The gruesome age in the history of books begins with the invention of that monster from Mainz, a monster whose name no living book will ever speak aloud at any price. The man had nothing better to do than to devise ways of easing and speeding up the manufacture of books—as if anyone had complained that the work was slow or difficult! For thousands of years books had been brought into this world by time-honored, tried and tested means, and no-one had objected. Everyone was happy, everyone was content, including us. And then this fellow got it into his head that the whole business was wrong, and that he would show us all how to put it right. And didn't he show us. For half a millennium our hides have taken the consequences of his invention.

Books were duplicated before, of course, but that was not cloning. Copies were similar but not identical. They were like twins growing from two ova. Same father, same mother, somewhat different children. A human hand, copying from another handwritten copy, can never achieve the same fidelity as the printing press, so each copy was unique and irreplaceable, exactly resembling no other.

And when something is unique and irreplaceable, its price is, naturally, all the higher. Oh, how humans used to respect and value us before they started printing us. What days those were! The abyss into which we were later to be thrown was unimaginable in the era before the malefactor of Mainz.

To begin with, there was no pandering to the public. None at all. The plague of general literacy was not yet let loose upon the world. We came into contact only with the most enlightened of the social elite. Only royalty, the nobility and the more respectable clergy took us into their hands—no-one from the lower echelons. We regarded ourselves therefore as in every respect a privileged class: an aristocracy.

As is usually the case with an aristocracy, its members were zealously guarded from the moment of their birth. Nothing was left to chance. Blue blood is pure blood, not to be mixed with the rabble. We were born only in royal courts (where we were mostly written) and in monasteries (where we were mostly copied), these being, indeed, the only oases of spirituality in that dark era.

Both at the time of our birth and during copying, we received the best of attention, as was our due. First came parchment, then papyrus, and then paper, but all were of great scarcity and cost. They were certainly not to be wasted on plot outlines, working versions and other clerkish scribblings without which one couldn't imagine even the most banal writing being produced today, when even a shopping list, for instance, will go through several drafts. Back then, authors adhered to the golden rule of tailoring: measure thrice to cut once.

They would consider every sentence three times over before writing it down.

It is no accident that literary works from those times are distinguished by their dignified sense of proportion—unlike today's prose, which you could cut in half without compunction and using the crudest formulae, such as doing away with every other page, or the whole first half of the novel. You can do so in the confidence that no-one, least of all the author, will ever notice a thing. That is what you get when whole forests are cut down and mercilessly pulped so that every insignificant human nobody can have at his disposal an abundance of paper, whereon to scribble whatever comes into his head. They count that, too, as a benefit of democracy.

The hand-copying, no less than the writing of an original, took a long time. There were no shortcuts. The hand which clutches a goose-feather quill cannot be hurried; in addition to all his other responsibilities, the scribe must dip the quill frequently into the inkpot, as well as sharpening it from time to time, because it tends to get blunt quickly. Then it leaves a thick, ugly trace, and there's a greater risk of making blotches. Add to that the constant dread of making a mistake which haunted author and scribe alike, the nightmare of their waking hours no less than of their sleep, which further slowed their work; there being no opportunity to make corrections, a precious page would have to be thrown away. This was the cause of many a nervous breakdown and even the occasional suicide. Thus one can see why the composition of one work of literature could consume a number of months, or (if the work was particularly voluminous) many years.

What a different story from the modern day, when anyone who wants to try his hand at being a writer can do so virtually free of cost—there's no cheaper art than this. The eager aspirant just strolls down to the nearest stationer's, buys as much paper as he wants for next to nothing, and then, without the least compunction, pulls out of his typewriter and tears up page after page the minute he takes the smallest dislike to anything he has written.

A comma, for instance. He just happens, quite fortuitously, to type a comma where he doesn't want one. That solitary piece of punctuation may as well just stay there; a comma more or less is hardly a big deal—it isn't as though all the others have been placed correctly! Or he could cross it out with a pencil and ignore it—but no, a whole sheet of paper must be sacrificed for the sake of a comma! This purist is capable of wasting a whole beech tree before completing a first page to his own absolute satisfaction. And why not? He can do whatever he likes.

Since the computer came along, all sense of proportion has gone out the window. True, beech trees are no longer put to the sword en masse, but there's a prodigal waste of electricity. Before finishing a first draft with all the corrections, re-writings, additions and deletions, the would-be literary lion expends more energy than a leading monastery in the Middle Ages spent on a whole year's candlelight and torchlight. And nobody takes any notice! Should they ever pause to reflect on the matter, the proud literati would simply wave it away—easy come (they would reason), easy go.

Maybe their arrogant nonchalance would be deflated if they were made to pass a single day as a scribe. Then they would see for themselves with what dedication, diligence and discipline—piety came with the territory—a monk approached the task of copying a book, which is to say, producing a new book.

Not everyone, for a start, even among the monks, was cut out for this essential and elaborate work. Only the most conscientious and industrious were chosen—those ready to give up their entire lives, without complaint or remonstration, devoutly and humbly as befitted the chosen servants of God, standing each at his own desk in the scriptorium and copying, with infinite care and patience, page upon page.

They might have been enabled to sit at their work, but too much comfort can make a man complacent, and where complacency takes root, the Father of Lies discovers his easiest prey. Then not only do involuntary mistakes and omissions creep in, but the sacred integrity of the original begins to be violated: unsanctioned changes are made in the holy text, or, worse still, additional words may start to appear. That had to be prevented at all costs, so it is small wonder if the monastic Fathers banned chairs permanently from the scriptoria.

So all day long, through the days and weeks and months, the monks stood up, while out in the wide world the seasons pursued their monotonous course, to amass with equal monotony the Years of Our Lord. Thus did they copy one manuscript after the next, adding each time an indispensable brick to the building of some monastic or royal library. So much standing resulted in flat feet. That was inevitable, but no-one minded at all. It was a far nobler infirmity than the one which afflicted the builders of literature in later ages—men who, before they had even entered middle age, fell victim through too much sitting at their desks to the humiliating affliction of hemorrhoids.

The working life of a monastic scribe had to come to an end when his sight deteriorated, as was the inevitable result of peering so much at tiny handwriting. Such veterans were highly respected and admired among the brethren. They were regarded almost as though ready for elevation into the Communion of Saints. But this did little to banish the feelings of uselessness and futility which engulfed them once they could no longer perform their elite function. In the end, only total surrender to their faith could bring them any measure of consolation.

What these scribes left behind as the token of their life's work is hardly impressive by contemporary standards. Fifty copies or so thrown out as spoilage—that's normal today, regular practice in a typical printing-house, even when the print-run is quite modest. But in the era before the invention of these terrible institutions, fifty volumes might be the fruit of one man's lifetime of devoted labor.

It is, then, entirely understandable that those who instructed our making by a monastery regarded us as chattels of the highest value. They knew all too well how painstaking, slow and costly was the production of a single book. For those possessors, we were rated no less than any other class of treasure. Moreover, unlike gemstones, precious metals and other valuables of a more durable nature, that needed only to be kept safe, we required special care owing to our fragility and general vulnerability to various ailments.

We were accommodated in dry places with an even temperature, often with our own valet, a man whose sole duty was to serve us and see to our every comfort. And when one of the few individuals so privileged wished to read us, they all, from the king down, were made to abide by a rigid protocol.

Reading could take place only in a special room, and under the most favorable conditions: appropriate warmth, low moisture, no dust or other pollutants; with all the windows closed, even in midsummer, so that nothing from outside could endanger us; the table where we were placed must be perfectly smooth, without any rough spots to abrade our binding. What's more, the reader was absolutely forbidden to touch us with his bare fingers; he had to wear gloves, which must be white of course, so as to harm us as little as possible when he turned our pages.

When the reading session finally came to an end, there was no way we could be left lying open on the table, nor could any other indignity befall us; nothing from the modern reader's inexhaustible repertoire of violent and filthy acts. The valet would come for us. He would first check very carefully to see that everything was completely right with us, and then he would bear us away to our well-earned rest within the confines of our private quarters.

The only real danger we faced in that happy era, our Golden Age, was fire. It was a rare occurrence, but unpredictable: fires were mostly attendant upon the invasion of savage hordes, erupting into civilized, orderly lands. In such cataclysms we were the first to perish. Although we did nothing to harm the barbarians, for some reason they targeted us first, ruthlessly burning vast libraries to ashes, and deriving great enjoyment from the spectacle.

How different from nowadays, when a massacre of books, by flame or other means, doesn't much upset (or much rejoice) any humans, but on the contrary, leaves them pretty indifferent. They know there's nothing easier than to print a few more copies. The waste of paper may be regretted but not much, since it isn't very expensive—whereas in olden days the burning down of a library was a real tragedy of national, even international, proportions.

Lost books were mourned almost as much as perished lives—occasionally more so, since some people, especially those belonging to the lower orders, might be said to have been, if not utterly worthless, then certainly not of much significance; but the loss of each and every book was, without exception, irretrievable. That's why historians attach the same importance to the sacking of a great library as to the downfall of a whole nation in the wake of the bloodiest of battles.

Every idyll has an end, however. No Golden Age lasts forever. Ours, if it is any consolation, lasted several thousand years: we lived them as a species of intelligence and nobility ought to live. Not in perfect ease and safety, no, but in comfort, enjoying respect and—there's no question of it—privilege. Aristocratically, in a word. And then an event rather common in human history took place. There was a revolution. The monster of Mainz turned book-making democratic—and everything has been downhill since then.

*(We had just started on a new paragraph lamenting the way this terrible revolution was instantly embraced by all humans, and how even our closest and most loyal companions turned their backs on us, when we remembered at the last moment that it wasn't quite as simple as that. Though that soulless species probably doesn't deserve such fair treatment, we will admit, for the sake of truth, that there were exceptions. We want to be even-handed. The exceptions were very rare indeed, and popped up in the most unlikely places, nevertheless, there were individual humans, and there are yet, even today, who did not readily accept the ghastly contraption of the criminal from Mainz; some who abhorred it, in fact, perhaps not as viscerally as we, but fiercely all the same. We are obliged in the service of objectivity, and by a certain degree of affection, to mention at least one of them. There recently fell to our notice the manuscript of a story entitled "The Captain's Library." Either out of modesty, or for some other reason, the author omitted his name, so that we are not in a position to verify the reality or otherwise of the tale. It may be entirely imaginary. We hope—in the name of preserving the last shreds of our once firmly-held belief that humans are not, morally, an entirely hopeless species—that the story is founded in truth. On the other hand, our whole recent experience warns us in the voice of thunder that it must be a complete and utter fantasy. We leave it to you to judge, having read the tale, which of these options seems the more probable. And so: "The Captain's Library.")*

The interior of the cabin door was entirely different from its outer appearance. Instead of crude, gnarled beech wood, it was all polished mahogany, inlaid with brighter materials and secured by ornamental brass fittings. A door in keeping with the quarters of a ship's captain who wishes to assert his uniquely superior status—even if his vessel is actually a pirate ship. And why should a pirate captain not appreciate beauty?

It is prejudice alone, in fact, which holds them to be savage, primitive cutthroats who belch at table, wipe their mouths on their sleeves and throw gnawed bones into every corner. Nothing could be further from the case! Among pirate captains one can find any number of individuals whose manners are truly refined, cultivated and polite; men who, moreover, are capable of appreciating and, often, of creating works of art.

Although you will certainly never discover as much in literary histories, since it would be unedifying to mention such distasteful realities, many a great poem and even several excellent novels were composed in just such cabins, during lulls between piratical or adventuring activities. Likewise there are countless still-lifes, some of which have found their way into the galleries of great museums, created in moments of inspiration after the division of booty valiantly liberated from possessors who, for obvious reasons, will have no further use for it. It is only natural that on such occasions the captains (at least those of finer sensibilities) are in no hurry to seize for themselves those trifles which fascinate the common crewmen and perhaps even the less educated officers. Gold and silver and other such obviously valuable items, don't have a great attraction for such captains; but a rare book or a painting by an old master can certainly appease a delicate conscience, troubled over the somewhat dishonest means by which they were obtained. In such cases, the ideal circumstance is for one pirate ship to rob another; the question of honest acquisition having been completely canceled out, the luckier and more capable captain can then enjoy his newly acquired riches with a quite easy mind.

That our present captain was of that special sort was demonstrated by numerous unmistakable signs within the cabin. Indeed, had it not been for a small, black, triangular gonfalon bearing the device of a white skull-and-crossbones, which stood on a heavy marble base upon his ample desk—a desk which required six legs, though slender, elegantly curved and ornately carved—one might have fancied that this room was the atelier or salon of a connoisseur who, for some eccentric reason, chose to dwell on a sailing ship instead of, as might have been expected, a remote castle surrounded by carefully tended lawns and hidden among shady evergreen forests.

It's another vulgar prejudice, however, to assume that true devotees of the arts invariably choose to retreat into such sheltered environs. Quite the opposite is true: you are more likely to find them in quite different places, some of which may not seem entirely suited to the contemplation of artistic beauty. Don't be deceived by appearances! Artistry and its appreciation may dwell where no-one suspects it might be found.

Even were you to overlook the white grand piano (on your right as you step through the door)—from which there sometimes flowed the strains of elegies of depthless melancholy, causing shivers of nameless dread to run through sailors unused to such sounds—and if you were to ignore the right-hand wall, almost entirely covered with winter landscapes, the best that could be obtained on the high seas, with frames curled into such arabesques as to provoke envy in even the haughtiest art-collector, it would yet be impossible to overlook the vast library ranged along the whole of the left-hand wall, from the ceiling timbers with their rounded wooden beams down to the brightly polished deck.

What a variety of bindings and spines were there to be seen! On the higher, less accessible shelves reposed the captain's favorites, ancient manuscripts from the days before printing, laboriously copied. The antiquities did not, in fact, possess any binding in the usual sense. Stiff leaves were held in place between thin tablets of stone or wood resembling rudimentary book-covers, without any semblance of a spine. Only by reaching down the book could one discover what it was, and that privilege was reserved to the captain alone. Should anyone else, out of unimaginable ignorance (or, worse yet, mischief) attempt to remove a book from this library, that miscreant would suffer immediate capital punishment, without hope of forgiveness or mercy. Not that such a thing had ever occurred; the inclinations of his crew lay in essentially different directions.

The next highest shelves of the library reflected the history of printing skills. A row of precious incunabulas, both tabulary and typographic, illustrated the work of the early printers, the problems they encountered and the stages of trial and error through which they overcame them. What materials had not been used for binding in those pioneering times? Anything, almost, which seemed of sufficient strength and durability might be employed, but leather above all.

Skin, in other words; torn from every imaginable species of wild and domestic mammal, and even a number of birds, processed and cured for the purpose. After almost a century of experimentation, it had been unequivocally proved that learned texts, whether religious or secular, are best encased in leather derived from boars which, having been gelded at an early age, are then allowed to roam for a time through a fenced-off area of an oak forest which is not too damp; while lighter volumes of a more emotional nature (a category which includes devotional poetry) are best clad in the leather of young pregnant cows, because of its lighter shade, and which will be found to lose none of its virtues even when the mood of the contents is predominantly pensive or even melancholy.

Among the uncouth and superstitious crewmen there sometimes—especially on nights when the moon was full—circulated whispers that among the captain's books were some whose leather originated from no animal at all. Brave and cruel as they were, hardened sailors who had each looked death in the eye on many occasions, they still shivered with horror at the thought that some of the volumes in the captain's library might actually be bound in human hide. Such rumors enhanced his authority no end, and induced the sailors to look with a certain awe upon the library, which might otherwise have become, together with any person known to cherish books, an object of sarcastic and irreverent remarks. Nothing encourages loyalty and discipline so well as the idea that the punishment for betrayal or insubordination might be so horribly and literally visited upon one's own skin.

Below the incunabulas and other early printed books were those rare folio editions in which the captain most frequently sought solace during the hours of somber lassitude which, as the years slipped by, came to bedevil him more and more. It is untrue to say that pirates, especially the more educated among them, recoil from the ultimate questions of morality, metaphysics and epistemology, particularly those which bear directly upon the meaning of life. Thinking of these matters, in the long and lonely hours when the ship lay becalmed, without a breath of wind to tighten her sails and drive them forward into new adventures, the captain came to evaluate most critically—harshly, even—the course of his own existence until then. At such times it seemed to him that he could discern very few, if any, moments when it had been touched by the sublime; which reflection offered so bleak a prospect for the times to come, that he was assailed by the darkest fears—even to the point of considering suicide as a means of slashing swiftly through the mire of futility which imprisoned him. Many pirate captains, shrinking from that irreversible step, seek oblivion in drunkenness, although it is well known that the false relief of such transient amnesia only leads deeper into the abyss. Many captains—but not this one.

When these dismal thoughts assailed him, the captain—upon whose six-legged desk hard by the small pirate's flag, on an old wooden bracket polished smooth with long use, there stood a sharply pointed hook, the only golden item in his cabin—used to seek salvation among those large tomes with the tissue-thin pages in which were preserved the complete works of the great literary masters. It was the only golden item in his cabin, and he would use it to seek salvation among those large tomes with the tissue-thin pages in which were preserved the complete works of the great literary masters. Although at times like these it would soothe him most to read about a kindred soul tormented by similar sorrows, he had long ago resigned himself to the knowledge that his honorable trade seemed rarely to offer inspiration to such writers. Indeed, few authors ever wrote about pirate captains, even about those redeemed by education; and those who did tended to do so without much understanding or affection. But there was nothing to be done about that: in a world so full of injustice, this latest example was a matter only for regret, not wonder.

He derived some consolation for the lack of texts about his quite unjustifiably neglected and undervalued profession in one kind of verse, which only seemed to be out of keeping with its harshness and brutality. In the harmonious rhymes of the sonnets, in the enchanting elegance of that poetic form, in the endless scope for ingenuity which it offers within such narrow constraints, and above all in the supremely delicate feelings described in exquisitely chosen words, he found such balm that he frequently read them aloud, in a state of rapture and with wild gesticulations, as if reciting for a large and eager audience.

Most affecting of all were the sonnets' concluding couplets; his tightly controlled voice would then waver with emotion, his eyes well up with tears. On certain occasions the tears would gush openly, unrestrainedly, especially when he chose to read the sonnets about his favorite heroine, the Dark Lady, who seemed (because of her melancholy coloring if for no other reason) the object most suited to his adoration. It would certainly not have done for some common seaman, or even officer, to see him in such a state; he had therefore given the most stern instructions that he was never to be disturbed by anyone while reading aloud, for any cause or on whatever pretext. In fact, his readings brought life to a standstill throughout the ship; everyone walked on tiptoe if they must walk at all, and such conversations as could not be postponed were carried on in whispers. The only insoluble problem was the totally inconsiderate screeching of the gulls, especially when the ship lay at anchor or was close to land; muskets and blunderbusses could not be resorted to because of the disproportionate noise they made, and none of the crew could boast the Ancient Mariner's skill with bow and arrow.

Below the folio editions were rows of books of more and more recent date. Although he had personally selected them, the captain accorded them less reverence than those works on the more elevated shelves. He was well aware that this laid him open to the charge of having old-fashioned tastes; a charge he did not bother to deny. Some of these younger tomes were no doubt works of genius; but they were rendered less worthy in his eyes by the fact that, as their provenance approached the present day, their initial print-runs grew ever longer and longer. That, in his view, was a quite lamentable desecration and profanation of an art which should have confined itself to an elite.

Occasionally a new edition of the Dark Lady sonnets came his way, and some of these new settings were more finely produced, more tastefully arranged than the first edition which he treasured so much, but he flung them overboard in disgust. He knew this was not a very reasonable attitude, since the text was exactly the same, even embellished with historical introductions, explanatory notes and learned commentaries, but he justified his actions by means of the ancient, unassailable truth that a book, after all, is more than just a text. What, apart from text, a book is, the captain could not perhaps have explained satisfactorily to anyone else, but to him it seemed too obvious to require explanation; hadn't it been observed long since that the most self-evident of truths are sometimes the most difficult to define?

In any case, the lowest shelves of his library, those below the knee, were occupied by books from the age when publishing had ceased to be a skilled craft and had become an industry. Although this part of the library was more colorful and lively-looking than the dull and predominantly grey upper ranges, the comparative disrespect the captain felt for it was expressed not only by the low place he assigned the books but also by a certain uncharacteristic neglect. While he took passionate care of the higher volumes, he allowed the bottom shelves to accumulate dust over long periods, quite deliberately, as if punishing them. And of course, at the very nadir, almost on the deck, were the editions which, by the captain's rigid criteria, were worthy only of the deepest contempt: the paperbacks. These were only dusted at the big spring-cleanings, which occurred but seldom.

THE MANUSCRIPT OF "THE Captain's Library," unsigned as it is, was submitted for publication. This we learn from the short note of a human, probably the editor of the Literary Supplement of some Sunday newspaper; his comments are added at the end of the manuscript. He rejected the story and briefly explained why.

The editor had no complaints about the quality of the story. He pointed out that the language was interesting, and the tone and theme were original as well. What stood in the way of its being published was what he described as "a certain unfinished quality." The ending of the story was somehow abrupt. The reader's expectations were in a way betrayed. The author should have added a paragraph or two, to explain what lay beneath the paperbacks, even if this required him to wrench up a plank from the cabin floor. There, supposedly, something of even lesser esteem must lie hidden.

No information is given as to whether the author followed this suggestion. From the fact that the story never saw publication, we may presume that he did not. Perhaps the editor's remarks struck him as inappropriate or even stupid. What, in fact, could be lower than a pocket paperback? Do they not represent the ultimate degeneracy wrought by the democratic revolution of the Monster from Mainz?

Actually, no. They don't!

Although the anonymous editor did not hint at the nature of the things which might, perhaps, lie hidden under the floorboards which formed the bottom-most shelf, his intuition did not lead him astray. The objects that might be stashed there, doubtless to hide their shame, and harboring a boundless hatred of books, are the heralds of yet another revolution in publishing, completely in tune with the spirit of modern times. This latest revolution is even more democratic than the previous one, the march in that direction having irresistible momentum if no final goal. It is a revolution poised to sweep the book entirely from the face of the Earth as an obsolete, redundant relic of the past, a pure anachronism. It has long been brewing openly and right before our eyes, but we, the books, have remained blind to it, just as we did during the invention of the printing-press; we hadn't the slightest inkling, let alone full knowledge, of what was going on.

Yet this we had to notice. All the signs of the revolution have been there, ever since the computer was invented. No species, especially not one which prides itself on its intelligence, should ever allow its survival instincts to wither. To be quite frank, this blindness may be the best confirmation yet that our time is really over, that we are finished.

This may be extremely painful and for us disastrous, but reality must be faced: in the near future, books will cease to be published any more. There will be no need for them. Our niche in the arena of evolution will be snatched and filled by a newer, more highly-evolved species. This takes place all the time, but one generally pays no attention while it is happening to others. Only when it starts to happen to you do you become truly aware of it. But by then your time is up. It's far too late.

We won't vanish overnight, though, like the dinosaurs. First we will disappear from the bookshop shelves, where our evolutionary inheritors will replace us; but for some time thereafter we will linger in the public libraries, until we are removed from those refuges because demand for us will have dropped to almost zero.

For a somewhat longer period we will survive in the private libraries of various eccentrics and weirdos, though with no influx of fresh editions, we will inevitably suffer a thinning of ranks even there. In the final stage, a few obsessive boffins or nostalgia buffs will still seek us out, but they will find us only in museums, in the galleries devoted to extinct species. Somewhere, let us say, between the mammoths and the pterodactyls.

It is quite unlikely that the museum's curators will bother to mention, even in the smallest print, that unlike our extinct neighbors in those lifeless and dreary chambers, we used to be an intelligent race, one of only two such breeds so far produced by terrestrial evolution. And no wonder: for human vanity, envy and rivalry are without limit.

Were our malice even remotely comparable to that of humans, we would wish the same destiny upon them too, when the bell tolls for humans to be consigned to the museums of natural history. Which is going to happen, whether they like it or not. No-one's evolutionary candle has ever burned through till dawn, and nor will theirs. But we are not like humans, of course. That is why, in parting, we wish them all the best. Good luck to them. And may their display cases be set up a long way away from ours.

*(Honored and patient reader, it remains to present to you one single episode of no great length. It is the sequel to our earlier description of a writer submitting his first manuscript for publication. The event described below might not merit comment—some readers may be quite capable of imagining it both accurately and in detail without our assistance—were it not that, at the climax of this very occasion we discovered the identity of the species which will soon replace us. Moreover, the affair was as lavish and glamorous as one could wish, being, as it was, the launch of the young author's novel. Fortunately, these bashes are cheerful and amusing get-togethers, so this narrative will end, not in a high tone of lamentation, nor with an air of elegy, nor even in the accents of grim foreboding. Rather, its conclusion will be serene, with just a touch of melancholy, in keeping with its general character up to this point. The voice, however, will be human once more. This is regrettable, but inevitable. Not only did he narrate the first part of the tale, making it unfair to say*

*the least, to deny him the opportunity of ending it, but also, a human word must be the last word in everything. There is no other choice, it is the way of the world, and it will be that much easier, therefore, for us to leave it. And so: The Launch.)*

The secretary does not like book launches in the least. Indeed, she hates them with all her heart. To begin with, they are always organized outside working hours, when she might be doing much more enjoyable things than hobnobbing with the tedious audience, the journalists who are forever asking inane questions, and the pompous speechmakers. The only question is which of them are the worst.

More than half the audience are people who happen to be there purely by accident: idlers who don't know what to do with themselves, are profoundly uninterested in the theme, and are only there for the purpose of killing time. Still, it gives them the illusion of participating in an important cultural event—at least until they doze off. Thereafter nothing matters much.

Some drop by for more pragmatic reasons. In winter it gives them an opportunity to get warm for free; in summer to cool down, likewise for nothing. The air-conditioning vent, looming above the bookshop door, is somewhat noisy, and a pool of water gathers underneath it, but it still gets switched on in honor of such occasions.

The rest are the relatives and friends of the author.

They are not at all difficult to identify. Their clothes betray their allegiance.

In summer the first group dresses casually, to put it mildly: shorts and T-shirts, in the main, or even no T-shirt when the weather is at its hottest. Most are licking ice creams, but a slice of pizza or a hamburger are not beyond them; in hot weather the best time for a snack is right now, in the early evening, when the food won't lie too heavily on the stomach. Besides, it's a well-known fact that intellectual effort makes you hungry. To aid the digestion, of course, something is needed to wash the snack down: some canned drink, cold and refreshing. It has to be carbonated. To finish off, by way of substitute for brushing their teeth, they never fail to use some chewing-gum.

But the real free-for-all begins when they take the trainers off their feet, so as to make themselves more comfortable while they listen, with eyes open or closed: if there have been any mosquitoes in the bookshop, those flying pests will now make a beeline for the exit as fast as their wings will go. It may not be generally known, but nothing repels those airborne vermin so effectively as the odor which rises from that type of footwear after a whole day on a bare foot in the hot sun.

Guests have been known to turn up straight from the beach, practically in their swimsuits—leaving a pool of water behind them on their chairs.

In winter they stomp in, their feet now covered by worn-out galoshes, trailing muddy footprints all over the bookshop, and for some reason they never remove their heavy sheepskins or their huge fur hats, as if they were setting off on an expedition to the Antarctic, rather than sitting in an overheated room.

Soon they are sweating and their faces are flushing up nicely; then steam begins to waft from them, as if they were sitting in a hot oven. But none of this will induce them to shed so much as a scarf. No, they wouldn't do so, though their lives depended on it. Maybe they've all had bad experiences, and still go in fear of having their precious items of apparel stolen, should they hang them on the coat-hooks close at hand.

Most of them come equipped with thermos flasks, and they never hesitate to help themselves to a few mouthfuls of hot beverage every now and then, or to offer some to their neighbors even though they never have more than one cup. There's no better safeguard against the common cold which, at that season, lurks around every corner.

Judging, however, by their occasional involuntary lip-smacking, by a certain glassiness which comes over their eyes, and, most of all, by the fact that, once the monotonous literary discourse has been continuing for some time their heads droop inexplicably forward, their chins coming to rest upon their chests—one might conclude that the hot liquid in the thermos was not, after all, straight coffee, nor innocent, unadulterated tea, as one might have assumed at first in one's naiveté.

The author's kith and kin are entirely different. They most certainly did not blunder in here by accident. For them, this gathering is a social event of great importance, almost the equivalent of a marriage, or if not that, then the marking of some numerically rounded wedding anniversary. Or, at the very least, a funeral. Pride swells hugely within them. They have been asserting for a long time that the author would go far, even though there were others who shook their heads skeptically whenever such a hypothesis was mentioned. Yet, optimistic as they were, they had not anticipated so magnificent a success. A celebrity launch! Nothing low-key about this!

Such being their estimate of the occasion, they dress up to it—very formally. In fact they overdress. Bowties everywhere, and patent leather shoes; crisply starched shirts, it goes without saying; a tuxedo or two can be spotted, even ambassadorial tails with a top-hat, malacca cane, monocle and white gloves, though this is now becoming a rarer sight. All the men are clean-shaven, even those who usually sport beards, and for many this was an opportunity for a haircut and a pomade.

The ladies are also dolled up for the big event: a new hairdo is obligatory, plus some new item of clothing, so that no-one can say they always appear in the same out-fit. What's more, they are done up like Christmas trees with precious stones and metals. Sparkling and glittering from head to foot, they have no need of fireworks. It's been a once-in-lifetime opportunity to exhume the family jewels from their boxes, chests and safes, to strut and show them off a little in the world—when else will they get the chance? Do they ever go out with anyone? To the cinema, maybe, once in a while; that's all. They don't recall when they last went to the theatre, and as for the opera, they've completely forgotten what that kind of venue looks like.

This part of the audience listens with rapt attention. Not a word escapes them. They gaze at the speakers avidly, and at times they cup a hand about their ear to amplify their hearing if, by some misfortune, they happen to be seated next to some inconsiderate dozer more noisy than most. Many of them have brought along notebooks and pens, in order zealously to record the promoter's words. Some, more inventive, bring mini cassette-recorders, and hold them high in the air, the better to catch the sound. A passerby, casting a casual glance into the bookshop at promotion time, might think a small group of ostriches had mingled with the audience.

In recent times, these occasions have begun to be immortalized more comprehensively, not only on audio, but on video cassettes as well. In earlier days there might have been only the occasional flash from the camera held by relative or journalist; but no photo can really stand up to a video recording. Thanks to technical advances, and the consequent widespread use of technology, the camcorder is now an inevitable ingredient of these gatherings.

Every self-respecting person will see to it that this ceremonial gets recorded on someone's video. If he doesn't possess a camcorder, and no-one will lend him

one, it's not a problem. There are professionals to provide the service. They're quite without prejudice, those
men and women who earn their crust recording important family events: they're normally hired for wed-
dings, christenings, birthdays and burials, but they'll
agree to attend a book-launch just as willingly. They
won't charge extra, either—why should they? This
shindig isn't illegal or offensive to public morals, it isn't
in some remote, hard to get at location, and besides,
there's bound to be some sort of buffet or a drink at
least.

The two halves of the audience keep exchanging
glances, but each sees the other through quite different eyes. Dressed as if for a carnival, the author's
friends and relatives warily and reproachfully eye the
rest of the crowd, displaying in no uncertain terms
what they think of their clothes and manners. Really, all this lip-smacking and clicking of tongues! And
snoring, in such a place (not to mention certain other
mostly involuntary sound-effects, which for the sake
of delicacy we'll refrain from naming). And to come
out half-naked, or swathed in layers and layers of thick
clothing—how is that supposed to look? This isn't the
waiting-room of a provincial railway station! And even
if it were, good manners would still be in order—all
the more so at a launch!

The casual visitors, meanwhile, are casting eager and
impatient glances at the friends and relatives, believing
that these are film actors or at least extras, who may
at any moment begin their performance. Admittedly,
none is mentioned in the program, but the publisher probably meant it to be a surprise. Who else would
these people be, so blatantly over-dressed and made-
up? Note, also, the strange, stiff poses they are all
maintaining, as though they were mime-artists. Their
scene will begin, no doubt, as soon as the speakers have
finished their monologues. An excellent idea: it's high

time someone did something to break up the monotony of these literary evenings, where nothing at all exciting ever happens.

The secretary loathes the journalists even more. They're a vain, conceited lot, forever demanding special privileges. This starts with seats at the launch. The front row always has to be reserved for them. This might be understandable if they were especially careful and attentive listeners. But no!

First of all, no journalist ever arrives on time. Fifteen minutes late or so is the norm; this is almost a matter of protocol. And when they do arrive, they don't seem to notice a launch is going on. Their chief priority is to tour the bookshop greeting everyone they know, even the barest, once-met acquaintance. They know all about good manners.

Then, neither quietly nor discreetly, they turn to whomever happens to be sitting or standing closest: someone who may or may not have been present from the beginning, but who was certainly there earlier than themselves. What sort of event is this? Who is the young author? Who is funding the launch? Who is the publisher? An invitation arrived, of course, at their office, with all this information written neatly and clearly upon it. The secretary mailed it herself; but in the general chaos which is the natural state of their professional no less than their private lives, they have lost or misplaced it somehow, in any case they couldn't lay hands on it today, and it's a good thing they managed to remember the place and time of the gathering. They often blunder into places where no event is taking place—not, at least, on that particular day.

They could have obtained the information more directly, though, since a complimentary copy of the book plus promotional material was waiting for them on their chair, but they crammed it all hastily into a satchel or suchlike, so as to clear a place for themselves to sit down;

and being in the satchel, it's no longer readily available. Besides, who wants to make a study of it right now? It's simpler and quicker to ask. So they jot down the muttered responses of a colleague. By now the journalist has more or less got into the swing of things. The scribbled notes will serve as the basis for his later article. If a mistake slips in, he can always blame the colleague who (deliberately, of course) misinformed him. It's par for the course: the guy works for a rival newspaper, and he wouldn't put such a deception past him.

As soon as they have fully informed themselves about the launch, they seek out the secretary. But theirs is the glazed, feverishly impatient gaze of the addict. If they don't get coffee within seventeen seconds, it'll be the end of the world. The coffee, needless to say, arrives in time, though the secretary is by no means delighted with her role as hostess. While she is concocting coffee in a small washroom (promoted for this occasion into a "tea kitchen"), she engages in embittered meditation, sometimes garnished with tears, on the unjustness of this world's arrangements. Was it for this that she passed that crash course in computing with flying colors—so as to drudge as a common coffee-maker, as a waitress?

The journalists drink up their coffee in a rush, greedily almost, slurping loudly because it's still too hot. And they have no compunction about lighting a cigarette along with the coffee, even though the bookshop is plastered in No Smoking signs. Even *Strictly No Smoking*. But this only applies to the common herd, of course, not to VIPs like them. Besides, who ever heard of having coffee without cigarettes?

Then, as soon as the last drops of black liquid have slid down their throats and the last whiffs of bluish smoke are up and out of their lungs, they cast a panicked glance at their wrists and start back, aghast. You're kidding! Is that the time? They're going to be late again! Briskly they bounce out of their chairs, waving their satchels; rapidly they tell the obliging colleague, who for some reason is still listening to the speakers, that they're terribly sorry, the launch has been really great, they *so* wish they could stay to the end, but it's impossible, they have somewhere else to be and they're late already—heavens, there are never enough hours in the day! Before they actually depart they must, of course, exchange valedictions with all their acquaintances. Manners must come first.

Of all the attendees at the launch, the speakers make the secretary the most nervous—perhaps primarily because she has explicit orders from the director to treat them with kid gloves; she must be all sweetness and light, though she saw through such people long ago and lumped them together under the same category with the authors. Birds of a feather, and she knows it. All just blabbing on about nothing and then expecting to get paid for it. Handsomely as well. A speaker at this kind of do gets the equivalent of her month's salary or more. It's hardly surprising if she feels peeved at them. Jealous as well, not to put too fine a point on it.

The writers might have done something a bit worthwhile, after all, they did invest quite a lot of energy in typing their product, and as a result there's a book, something you can touch and feel the weight of—not that she likes to touch books, but all the same—while these fine fellows just walk in off the street as it were, and make some noise, crank their hurdy-gurdy a few times, for half an hour or so, no more—and probably less. Lots of difficult high-falutin' words, oozing buckets of pseudery, pompous chin-wagging galore. A sentence begins and it has no object in mind, no possible end in sight. It just goes on twisting and turning, slithering and snaking on, the head bearing no relation to the tail.

Nonetheless, the speechifying once over, the audience applauds without restraint. They clap until their palms are red and sore. A standing ovation, in fact! Dare they admit, in all honesty, that they didn't understand a word of it? If you were to demand that any one of these listeners summarize for you what the promoters have actually *said*, they wouldn't be able to utter a syllable. But this, it seems, is how it is meant to be when academic topics are discussed. Anyway, the speeches were so eloquent and fluent, so mellifluous; how could a person not clap, regardless of whether they have understood? Juries award points for artistic impression, do they not?

Once you've heard the promoters on several successive occasions—as she has had to do, it being a part of her job description to attend these shows, even though she doesn't get paid overtime, or a bonus for extra-mural activities, but has to make maybe fifteen coffees, wash up glasses in cold water, and without any rubber gloves either—whether you like it or not you realize that the speakers are repeating themselves, as if turning out speeches from an identical mold, or like a gramophone record jumping into the same groove over and over; only the title and the name of the author differ. The address is vague enough to apply to any book, which means they don't actually need to read it at all in order to be able to talk about it with authority.

The secretary knows this better than anyone. On several occasions she has failed to send the book to a promoter, or failed to send the right one, the one that was supposed to be the subject of discussion. No wonder; she has so many jobs to do, she's under so much stress she doesn't know whether she's coming or going, everything is expected of poor her and her alone, and with no help, not the tiniest bit of help, from any quarter.

But these oversights are never noticed. Both the promoters, the one who hasn't read anything at all and the other one who has probably read a book but the wrong one, perform completely convincingly, so that the audience go home believing that the two men were thoroughly informed and really knew what they were talking about. How could it be otherwise? They are high-minded and responsible people.

Only in such exceptional circumstances is she prepared less grudgingly to acknowledge the promoters' skill, even to find some hint of justification for their astronomical fees.

As for the promotion of *The Rotten Ghost of the Monastery*, a full seven days before it was due to be held the secretary knew it would not go the usual way. The director had solemnly informed her that he himself intended to participate and, moreover, as the sole promoter. This was a very rare event. He had attended almost all these gatherings, usually as an observer, but very correctly turned out, with a tie, even in the hottest weather. Shaving was *de rigueur*. He had to make some sacrifices for the sake of his business reputation.

In such circumstances, he became unusually generous: anyone at all important could count on coffee. Promoters definitely, journalists if they liked, and even the author himself, if it couldn't be avoided. That filled the secretary with bitterness, of course. She felt most unjustly neglected and exploited. Not so much because she had to make all those coffees—though that certainly contributed to her discontent—but mainly because, if she wanted to drink coffee at her own workstation, she had to bring it from home, at her own expense. Including the sugar. Water and cups she was free to use, of course. Thrifty he may have been, but the director was not a Scrooge.

Round about the same time as he announced his involvement in this particular promotion, another highly unusual event took place, though the secretary did not immediately notice any connection between them. Someone resembling a complete down-and-out barged into her office. He was young, perhaps no more than twenty, his shoulder-length hair all greasy and tangled, his beard straggly and unkempt, his glasses metal-framed with small round lenses. His jeans were so faded as to be almost transparent in places, his trainers also badly worn and wrongly laced. He carried a largish school bag, curling at the corners and plastered all over with luridly colored stickers. He was, unmistakably, a would-be writer.

The director had told her he was expecting a significant visitor, so she greeted this scarecrow with a withering stare. What would the important gentleman, whose arrival was imminent, think of their respectable publishing house if he encountered this ragged hobo in her office? And what was this creep thinking of, anyway? Did he imagine that anyone who felt like it could just walk in off the street on a whim, as if the place were an amusement park? Wasn't there a warning, printed large and clear, immediately beneath the name of their firm: "No Admittance to Uninvited Authors!"

She was just about to lay into the unsavory hack, when the director materialized at the door of his office. This scared her for a moment: now he would be angry with her for allowing this drifter to hang about the room—but the director's face broke into a smile. From ear to ear! She couldn't remember when she'd last seen him looking so delighted. Spreading his arms, he approached the newcomer as though greeting a long-lost brother, draped one arm about his shoulders and, oozing bonhomie, led him into the office.

The secretary remained standing where she was, her mouth agape, utterly disconcerted. Surely this couldn't be the significant visitor? She had imagined some sleek businessman, perhaps a literary agent. But just look at this creature! He must be some sort of cousin. What else? From the sticks, of course. The director was born in some rural backwater, so it was no wonder. But still, the guy could have made himself a bit more presentable. This wasn't the outback!

Nevertheless, she had little time to stand gawping. Before she could sit down in her upholstered chair, the director reappeared at the door and placed an order reserved exclusively for very important visits: "Two coffees. Strong."

She hurried off to make them, but when she came back, she almost dropped the tray and its two heavily steaming cups. She couldn't believe her eyes. The grubby fellow was crouching by her desk, tinkering away at the computer. He was using a screwdriver! And pliers! She wanted to say something, but her voice failed her. Her throat was tight, her vocal cords refused to resonate. She just looked on impotently while he continued dismantling her workstation and taking the parts into the director's office—with no more explanation than a bailiff's officer making a repossession.

Finally no trace of hardware remained on her desk. For a few long moments she gazed at this newly created wasteland, and was unable to restrain her tears. Must she be demoted so brutally? And for what reason? What had she done wrong? Had she not done her job conscientiously, enthusiastically too, from the very start? She even passed the course on her first attempt. And now some ignoramus, some greasy geek, would take her place just because he was related to the director!

But just wait, he'd see when the first book covers came up. He wouldn't know how to switch the computer on, let alone be able to produce anything. Then he'd try to coax her, ingratiate himself with her, for the sake of a little help; but no dice. He could stand on his head—she wouldn't lift a finger to assist him. The director could threaten to fire her, but she'd still show no mercy. The place would go to wrack and ruin without her, but that would serve the director right for treating her in such a mean and dastardly manner.

At length she managed to compose herself somewhat, she dabbed the tears from her eyes with a handkerchief and brought the coffee into the director's office. Head held high, she was the image of pride and dignity; no way would she let them see how hurt and insulted she was by this injustice, so that they could gloat and glory as men do when they have power over a defenseless woman. But a big surprise awaited her inside. It was terrible!

The computer lay in the middle of the director's desk, and the geek was still dismantling it further. The housing was off, and he was now poking around in the interior, disconnecting wires and other parts, as though he were back in his home village and cleaning the guts from a freshly slaughtered pig. She felt a quivering, a trembling inside her, it was rising and taking her over. She could have fainted at any moment, so nauseating was the spectacle. She never had been able to stand the sight of blood, which was why she had rejected her mother's advice to go into nursing. She somehow managed to put the tray down on a corner of the desk, and walked out, her hand over her mouth.

Seated alone at her empty desk, her expression a helpless stare, she fell prey to the darkest possible thoughts. She felt as though she were waiting outside an operating theatre in which some witch doctor or quack was slicing open her child. Her only child—her son! The operation took a long time, it seemed to go on forever. Ominous ripping and snapping sounds came from inside the room, freaking her out even more. She wrung her useless hands and bit her lip.

Finally the door opened, and the shabby relative strode in, bearing the reassembled computer; after him came the director, cradling the monitor in his arms almost as though embracing it. She remained motionless, unable to rise. Her premonitions were of the worst, but she was trying to read the outcome of the surgery from their faces. No sob escaped her throat, though it remained there poised and ready.

The men's faces were serene, even joyous. She couldn't read the geek clearly, but the director wore a particular facial expression seen only on the completion of an especially lucrative deal. Nothing lifted his customary anxious frown so effectively as an intimation of profit soon to be realized. Her anxiety, panic even, yielded now to puzzlement. What could this mean?

The country cousin approached with the computer and set it back in its old place on the desk by the monitor. The bum then spent a minute or two reconnecting cables, pushing each connector into its proper socket. Finally, he turned it on. The secretary had the irresistible impression that the whole office was reverberating to the thump of her heart. This was the moment of truth. Now all would be revealed: the outcome of this major surgery.

A few moments were supposed to elapse before the monitor lit up; now they seemed to stretch for an eternity. Then, at long last, a picture formed and lingered steadily on the screen. The secretary watched it with an unblinking stare, trying with all her might to spot anything out of the ordinary, but nothing seemed to be wrong. Everything appeared just fine. A great sigh of relief escaped her, but the relief was soon tempered by a series of perplexing questions.

What did it all mean? First they took the computer off her, then they returned it. Why? What had they done to it in there? And who was this guy, anyway? Maybe he wasn't a country cousin out to steal her job. Jeepers, what sort of people was the director starting to hang out with? Could this be something illegal? People had told her, quite nicely, that she should stay away from publishing, that there was always something shady going on—even more than in other lines of business. Why did no-one ever explain anything to her? She deserved at least that much: she had the right to an explanation.

Right on cue with her last unspoken question, the young man opened up a small plastic box and took out a round silvery plaque, flashing with reflected light. He bent closer to the computer tower and pressed a button; just above the button something emerged from the computer in response, something that protruded and looked to her like a small squarish tray—or a tongue. This had definitely not been there before. So. They had built this new thing into the computer. But what was it for? Did she need it?

The button was pressed again and the little tray withdrew inside, taking with it the shiny disk. A moment later, one very small green light twinkled, a low hum was heard and the screen suddenly came to life. Two neighboring pages of a book were seen, along the margins of which a millimeter or two of the book's edges and spine were hinted at. The secretary seated herself a little closer and concluded that this was quite convenient for reading. Just as if a real book were in front of her. No difference. While she was looking, the youth pressed one key on the keyboard and the two pages were replaced on screen by the next two, as if he had turned a page.

She was impatient to ask a crucial question, but the opportunity did not immediately present itself. The mysterious scruffy man stowed his tools in his bag, bowed curtly towards her, shook hands with the director, who was still the very image of amiability, and left.

Only after the door had closed behind him did the secretary finally utter, in hesitant, somewhat fearful, even plaintive tones: "What is this?"

"The future," replied the director concisely, and disappeared back into his office with the spring in his step of a man who has seen a vision.

THE SECRETARY—ALONG WITH THE rest of the world—will be privileged to share the vision of the future only at the launch of *The Rotten Ghost of the Monastery*. The audience gathered for this event, very much the usual crowd of friends and ne'er-do-wells, may not notice anything odd, but the secretary's sharp eye catches a series of peculiarities setting it out of the ordinary; making it, for good reason, a unique—even epochal—event.

To begin with the most superficial of factors, the director's clothes and his general appearance. For this occasion he has put on his most formal suit, the one he reserves only for especially important funerals and for his rare trips abroad. In the secretary's opinion, this suit represents a new low in chic, style and cool, though she has taken great care to prevent her employer from ever discovering that. Really, of all the colors available, how could he choose this loud violet stripe? And then there's the cut. It's like a parody of a gangster movie. Everything is too wide for him, which means that everything flaps, making him look even chunkier and bulkier than he is by nature. But every time he starts marching and strutting back and forth in front of her in that clownish get-up, she lets him have the expected compliment. A bit of sucking up never does any harm.

An overall improvement in appearance is required to offset such clothes, of course. The director went to the barber's first and got a brutally short haircut, like a newly inducted rookie, but that's still better than the time he tried to grow his hair long, on which occasion his head, being in a state of well-advanced baldness up top, took on the appearance of a mangy ceiling-duster. Next he visited a manicurist, a move of which the secretary—a person greatly devoted to the tending and cultivation of various parts of her own body—approves.

Even so, she doubts whether this will bring about any permanent improvement, owing to the generally neglected state of his fingers, made worse by his tendency to bite his nails like a teenager, despite the fact that he is well into middle age.

Today the icing on the cake is the scent. The secretary estimates that he must have steeped himself in no less than a third of a standard bottle. It must have contained the very attar of violets, because no sooner had he arrived than the entire bookshop began to smell like a May meadow. Those in his immediate vicinity show signs of imminently passing out on account of this smell which, mingled with the powerful deodorant he uses to counteract the excessive sweating typical of plump people even when the room is not warm, is strong enough to etherize. Luckily there are no other speakers; he has the podium to himself. It's unlikely that anyone would have been able to sit next to him without requiring mouth-to-mouth resuscitation at regular intervals.

The snacks are also exceptional at this launch. Coffee is available in such quantities that there's even some for the audience. The secretary has accepted with relief and gratitude the director's suggestion that on this particular occasion she should be spared the duty of coffee-making. Had a waitress not been hired from a nearby restaurant to perform this task, the secretary wouldn't have had a chance to emerge from the washroom, and so would have been prevented from hearing the director's historic speech.

In addition to this, a precedent has been set that could previously only have been envisaged at a book fair. The director has loosened the last of his purse-strings and purchased a bottle of some kind of strong liquor. A *medium-sized* bottle. A good part of the audience would have preferred this congenial potion to any coffee, had the choice been offered them, but it has not. Precedents or no precedents, one mustn't overdo things. Only the journalists could count on a tot of it (or at most two). Anything more might render them insufficiently receptive to the director's great revelation.

During the preparations for the launch, the secretary noticed how keen the director was this time to secure the maximum possible press attention. The usual invitation cards, so subject to being mysteriously lost, were insufficient for this occasion. She had to call up each and every journalist on the phone as well, entirely suppressing her understandable distaste toward the species. In her most obsequious tones she requested them, if at all possible, to be on time. As a final insurance, she repeated the invitation, in the same tones, on the very morning of the launch. And not without cause: the congenital forgetfulness of journalists has been notorious time out of mind. More than half of them could remember nothing of the first phone call.

Eventually this persistence paid off. Almost all the invitees appeared at the bookshop—and, most surprising of all, on time. This punctuality was no doubt assisted by the fact that the gathering was delayed for half an hour, not so much because of any cunning foresight on the director's part, but rather because the audience, hearing about the unlimited free coffee for all comers, rushed in a body for the washroom. The press of demand instantly overwhelmed the supply, so a second coffee-girl had to be drafted in from the restaurant.

This most welcome news soon spread beyond the bookshop, which rapidly became packed to the rafters. Certain individuals appeared who were seldom or never seen at such promotions, but they easily blended in with the other casual visitors; consequently the casuals soon outnumbered the author's friends and relatives.

This casual set's driven determination to stick it out to the end, come what may, despite having consumed several cups of coffee apiece, was decisively bolstered by a new rumor to the effect that, after some brief speech-ifying, a powerful alcoholic drink would also be hand-ed out for free, and in unlimited quantities—but only to those who had been present from the beginning. These hopes were encouraged by the sight of a still-un-opened bottle and a row of small glasses on a side table. Soon the more knowing individuals were asserting, with quiet confidence, that an entire crate of the same beneficial liquid had been spotted in the washroom.

Only the writer was somewhat disappointed in his expectations from the start of the launch. As the star of the evening, the man whose work was to be cere-moniously promoted, he had arrived looking fit for a parade—so much so that the secretary at first failed to recognize him. She didn't remember him too well in any case—who could commit every author to memo-ry?—so she had to try hard to find out who among the small crowd of overdressed relatives and friends was the valiant begetter of *The Rotten Ghost of the Monastery*.

After a while, good old female intuition enabled her to select him accurately from a group of similarly spruce young men. He had been strutting along the gondola bookshelves for an hour before the promotion started, looking down on the world as from a celestial height. He alone could possibly be the author! That one with the long white silken scarf around his neck.

It's extraordinary the lengths of self-sacrifice authors are prepared to go to in order to fulfill their own pre-conceptions of how someone in their profession is sup-posed to look. The female readiness to suffer for the sake of fashion is nothing in comparison to theirs.

Never mind the murderous heat in the shop caused by yet another breakdown in the air-conditioning. The repair firm was the victim of yet another strike, right now in the middle of a heat wave. For two months the workers had not been paid their hot meal bonus, and as by the nature of their work they were constantly exposed to the cold, their health had thereby been jeopardized. If the author firmly believed that it would be inappropriate for him to appear in public without a long white scarf, he would not be deterred by such a trifling circumstance as the temperature, which had now risen to just above forty-three degrees centigrade—and that was in the more shady areas of the shop.

Although he had never before attended a launch, the author did somehow assume that some time would be allotted for him to speak. This struck him as only right and natural. He would surely be expected to say something on his own behalf. Fair enough, he probably ought not to interpret his own book, though he wouldn't object to doing so if asked. For some reason he couldn't quite believe that the critics would do a satisfactory job, even if the back cover of *The Rotten Ghost of the Monastery* declared with all eloquence that he had their full support.

But at the very least he'd be expected to read an excerpt! He had been practicing for it—in front of the mirror, of course—these last several days. He had even briefly contemplated taking a few lessons in stage acting, or at least elocution, but had discovered that it is quite difficult to find instructors in those disciplines during the summer. That's their dead season, when they all disperse and make off for the seaside or wherever; so he had to rely on his own natural talents.

His expectation had been that someone would invite him to sit behind the speakers' desk; the secretary, presumably, she being the only one who knew him apart from his literary agent, who was not, after all, one of the organizers of this event. But all he got from her was a dark look accentuated by raised eyebrows, which left him puzzled. What did she find wrong with him now? Irresistibly, the first idea which occurs to all men when faced with that kind of reproachful stare from a female is: Have I forgotten to zip my fly? Fortunately a quick, not too discreet examination proved that this was not the case.

The time for speculation was then over, as a heavy-set, profusely sweating man, clad all in violet, was striding towards the speakers' podium. The author had no clear grasp of who the person might be, but it seemed to be some official, perhaps the master of ceremonies; so he approached the man. But not too closely. What kept him at a distance as surely as the same magnetic pole, was the overpowering scent of violets, combined with some heavy deodorant; oxygen being very poorly represented in the mix.

Struggling valiantly not to start coughing as he had that day in the secretary's office, which would totally scupper his participation in the evening because those coughing fits of his might last up to half an hour—he somehow managed to croak an introduction; though this expedient seemed unnecessary, since surely everyone here must recognize him by now. Who else was he likely to be, at a time like this? Then he asked where he might find a place for himself. He had good reason to be uncertain, because behind the desk and microphone there was only one chair, just now creaking uneasily as the massive, violet figure settled into it.

The man looked up at him as though briefly confused by the question, then, in an impatient undertone, told him to sit anywhere, but fast, the launch must begin, it was running late already. The author blinked at him uncomprehendingly for a few moments, then, having no better option, turned and looked for a spare chair in the audience.

Unfortunately, because of the unexpectedly huge turnout, all the seats were already filled, as were the aisles between the gondolas; in some places the people were packed together like bus passengers in the rush hour. So the author was obliged to move a long way from the speakers' podium, all the way to the washroom tea-kitchen, the only free space left because of the extra heat radiating from the electric hotplates, where coffee was still being made.

His initial humiliation at having to occupy such a place was mitigated to some extent by the reflection that, at this distance, he would at least be spared the sickening smell that was catching the back of his throat.

At last there were no further obstacles and the event could begin. The director tapped the microphone with his finger to check whether it was switched on, slightly loosened his tie (green, with yellow polka-dots) to ease his breathing, and began:

"Honored guests! The book for which we are gathered here in such remarkable numbers, in this sultry weather . . ."

Here he paused, trying to remember the title, and failing; so he stuck his hand into the broad pocket of his violet jacket, pulled out a copy, cast a glance at the front cover, smiled as he turned it toward the audience for a moment, stuck it back in his pocket and continued:

" . . . *The Rotten Ghost of the Monastery*, written by our young author . . ." whom he tried to locate but could not see, the washroom being behind him—"is a very important one, we might say: an historic edition from this publisher."

A fresh pause, calculated to heighten the dramatic tension. One must be judicious with oratorical devices at any public appearance, most especially in hot weather.

"Not so much because of the book's own qualities, undeniable as they are. The critics have already given their approving, even flattering judgments on this work, a work that has already won a prestigious literary award."

In the general hullabaloo surrounding the preparations for this gathering, he had had very little time for details, and had forgotten to memorize exactly which award the secretary had chosen. This, too, was displayed on the front cover, but he had failed to note the information just now, and it would be awkward to pull the book out again just for that. Besides, it was of no import. The book would be completely forgotten soon enough.

"*The Rotten Ghost of the Monastery* will be primarily remembered as the last book ever to be produced by this publisher!"

On hearing this announcement the journalists in the front row, enjoying the privilege of being cooled by the one, chugging fan, jerked out of their absent-minded torpor. This might, contrary to all expectations, turn out to be an interesting day. Nothing creates more stir in the Culture pages than news of the downfall of a publisher. If it is coupled with a scandal, perhaps with a little bloodshed (not necessarily fatal) the story might even make the headlines.

Unfortunately, as if reading their thoughts, the director immediately crushed their sanguine hopes.

"But have no fear! We are not going out of business, as some might have initially assumed. Quite the opposite. We are pioneering a new chapter in the history of publishing!"

The newsmen's faces immediately dropped. With all due respect to the history of publishing in general, and new chapters in particular, that would hardly get the heads turning. Scandal is scandal, and readers love it, especially in summer, lying on the beach.

But the director did not let the **the lackluster response of the journalists deter him. He pressed on, with a vigor befitting the importance of his subject.

"We must keep pace with the times. The third millennium is about to begin. A new age is dawning, and shall publishing alone enter it in old clothes? In a form essentially unchanged for more than five hundred years? Maybe someone will remark at this point:

If something has not changed for so long, isn't that the best evidence that it is well designed, and should not be tampered with?

"But is that really the case? Is everything in publishing organized so well that it cannot be improved? Let us consider the very essentials of publishing first.

"What is the basic unit of publishing?"

This question was not directed at anyone in particular, but while he was asking it the director was looking at a group of listeners pressed between two gondolas, and for this reason several pairs of shoulders there shrugged to indicate that, in all sincerity, they hadn't the slightest idea what the correct answer might be.

"The book, of course!" was the director's enlightening explanation, after an appropriate rhetorical delay.

"And what is a book, essentially?" The director made a grand gesture with his arm, directed at the shelves crammed with tomes of all descriptions.

"Nothing but a mere repository of written words. A crude image for this would be a box full of some sort of text. A package, so to speak. Perhaps this will sound like sacrilege to some sensitive souls; like blasphemy, maybe. But a person like myself, whose profession is making books, cannot afford to have any illusions about them."

Here the director endured several suspicious, not to mention cutting looks which flashed at him from the better-dressed section of the audience, from people who were obviously not prepared for such a turn of events.

"We must inevitably ask ourselves whether that box is the best solution available to us. Doesn't it, perhaps, possess a few drawbacks?"

For an enhanced effect, the speaker waited a few moments more, although it was clear, of course, that no-one would answer him.

"It does, of course," he answered himself. "And more

than a few. The biggest of which is undoubtedly the material of which books are made: namely, paper.

"Is there, really, anything so frail and ephemeral as paper? You could hardly find anything to compare with it. Here, see for yourselves."

Then he reached into his pocket again, and took out the copy of *The Rotten Ghost of the Monastery*. To general surprise, and even a few shocked cries, he took a page and in one easy motion plucked it whole out of the binding.

"There, see. Should this"—he swung the paper rustling through the air—"wrestle with time? If not with eternity, which is what the author counts on. Nothing shorter interests him, and he has his reasons. Should it even be pitted against a normal human lifetime, as buyers rightly demand? Should they invest money in something which will not even outlast themselves?

"And I can guarantee you that it won't. You can have complete confidence in my rich experience of this matter. I know nothing so well as I know books. After all, I make books. Hardly a year will pass, and these pages will become all yellowed and withered. Another year, and the covers will pale completely and wear out. Then the glue will perish, and they will detach themselves from the rest of the book. Finally, as the third year expires, the binding will come unstitched, or will just fall off, so that there will be nothing to hold the leaves together any more. That which remains will hardly be worthy of the name of 'book.'"

The more convincingly to illustrate this grim destiny, the director continued to dismember *The Rotten Ghost of the Monastery*. As in time-lapse photography, the copy first lost its covers, then leaves flew from the binding, scattering themselves on the floor around where the speaker sat. Having discarded the last of the pages, so condensing three years into half a minute, the director rubbed and clapped his hands together to remove the dust, while wearing an expression of profound disgust.

The audience took this demonstration in two ways. One, smaller contingent looked on in mute horror, while the other, larger one regarded what they had seen as witty entertainment, possibly the warm-up to the second, less formal part of the evening, something they awaited with impatience and thought might begin any minute.

"Of course, books could be made from higher quality paper. I don't deny that. Then they would last somewhat longer, although still much less long than is desirable. But that is not the entire trouble with paper. Have you ever asked yourself how many trees must be felled for even one small print-run?"

This question was asked in an accusing tone, so that those swept by the director's angry look instinctively bowed their heads and lowered their gaze, although they couldn't quite discern wherein their personal guilt might lie.

"I'll tell you, if you haven't heard. A whole small copse of trees!"

He stopped, to let these words resound deeply even in the remotest cranny of the bookshop, like some evil omen.

"And forests are, as we all well know, the only source of oxygen on this planet. Each tree felled means less air for all of us now, and less, too, for later generations. We may say, in fact, that the appearance of each new book is another brick laid in the road leading to inevitable ecological disaster! And we have been publishing books like lunatics for hundreds of years already, caring nothing for the consequences, and with growing recklessness in modern times. There are far too many publishers and printers, for the sake of whose insatiable hunger for paper, everything alive has been cut down. They advance like termites, leaving nothing but barren wasteland in their wake. And when the reckoning is made, as at last it must, maybe we'll blame the whole thing on the Devil!"

A visible commotion was beginning to stir the more conscience-stricken segment of the audience. No-one had any inkling, of course, that the situation was so serious, that disaster lay already on the doorstep. Someone should have given a timely warning, so they could have taken steps to prevent the cataclysm. Perhaps they would even have stopped reading, if there really was no other remedy. The sight of so many books looming over them from the tall shelves suddenly seemed to them like a threat, the portent of a near-future world where people would lie gasping for a little air, helpless as fish whose pond has evaporated.

Unlike them the other, more relaxed contingent received the revelation without flinching. They had heard nothing new today. They had known for a long time that general disaster lay around the corner—and not just this disaster of deforestation, but a horde of other, far worse catastrophes. Everything's going to hell faster and faster, there's nothing to be done about it, so why ruin the time you have left moping over some stupid trees and oxygen somewhere? Big deal! Eat, drink and be merry. With any luck this speechifying will end soon (it's been going on too long already) and people will be able to wet their whistles. It's such muggy weather today. Especially here inside.

But the director, unfortunately, had no intention of ending his peroration.

"The stuff it's made of is not the only shortcoming of this box. Its holding capacity is woefully inadequate. Notwithstanding its bulkiness and heft, it can accommodate only a very modest amount of text. A measly thousand pages—and already you have a swollen, overweight book, almost fit for use as an offensive weapon. Indeed, it's a little known fact that several murders have been committed with a tome as the blunt instrument."

For a moment, in a flash of inspiration, the director thought of taking a large, hard volume from a nearby shelf—an illustrated art history, for instance, that would do nicely—and with the help of a volunteer, perhaps the author of *The Rotten Ghost of the Monastery*, demonstrating how easily murder can be committed using a book.

But to look convincing, this act would have to have been rehearsed, especially the collapse of the victim felled by a tome to the head. As there'd been no time for preparation, it was preferable to abandon the idea; it might lead to unforeseen consequences in any case. Besides, who knew what the audience would make of the performance. First you tore up the guy's book, then you murdered him, if only in play. Not really the ideal way to treat a guest.

"While the whole world aspires toward miniaturization, condensing more and more into an ever smaller space, no such thing is possible with books. We might produce really small books, no bigger than a fingernail; it has been done, but only as a bizarre gimmick, because who would read them? People's eyesight is deteriorating, every other person already wears spectacles, and when we use a small font even in a normal book we're inundated with complaints. Nobody's going to use a magnifying glass, even for a short while, it's as simple as that. For all we know magnifying glasses might be infected with the plague. No, that avenue of progress is a dead end."

A deep sigh, escaping the director at this point, was supposed to emphasize the inescapability of his conclusion.

"The book as a box for storing text is obviously a blind alley. No improvements or frills will help it any further. We must accept that fact, however terminal it may seem.

We need an entirely new box, unburdened by the failings of the previous one. The crucial question is: does such a box exist? Is there an alternative to the book?"

At this point came an inevitable pause. As a naturally gifted speaker, the director was well aware that at certain moments a little silence is worth a thousand words. The clearest confirmation of this came not so much from the better-dressed part of the audience, for whom it was natural to become all ears in feverish expectation of the sequel, but rather from the ranks of the casual visitors. It came also from the newsmen, who until then had concentrated exclusively on staring blankly ahead, some of them dozing more or less audibly, or quietly chatting with neighbors, or pursuing distant thoughts. A surprising number of them awoke to the sudden silence and stared in amazement at the speaker, wondering why there was no applause if the speech was finished.

Before continuing, the director first placed a hand unobtrusively in his pocket, but not the same pocket from which he had taken the book. He removed a small object which the audience could not see because he concealed it with his massive paw. It was a fitting introduction for what was to follow.

"Of course there is an alternative! An excellent one! A miraculous product of top-notch technology, a true herald of the coming age!"

The director's pause was shorter this time, just long enough to fit an appropriate frame around the historic announcement.

"What are the advantages of this powerful descendant of books? To begin with, it is not made of paper. It is constructed from a special kind of plastic, guaranteed to last practically forever. The future buyers of this product can rest assured that it will outlive them, no matter how long-lived they intend to be. In all probability the authors will be completely satisfied, although, for obvious reasons, no test has yet encompassed the whole of eternity.

"Next, the thing is molded as a single, seamless piece. There is nothing to go yellow or fade, to wilt, come unglued or unstitched or deteriorate. What's more, this product is resistant to most of the enemies of books, most notably to moisture—indeed, to water. If you want, you can keep it submerged in a vase of water, and no harm will come to it. When you wish to use it, you just wipe it clean and dry, and it is ready.

"Heat cannot harm it either—within limits, of course. In any case, the temperature at which this plastic begins to warp and melt is much higher than the burning-point of paper.

"The only real danger to this new invention is crude mechanical damage. Put it under a steam-roller, for instance, or hit it with a hammer, or apply an electric drill to it, and it will surely be ruined, but what other product, we ask ourselves, would survive such violence? Besides, the future users of this invention will be enlightened people, from whom we cannot expect the vandalism characteristic of people living in the era of the book. We can hope to have become a little wiser, a little nobler, in the interval."

The mildly reproachful tone in which he pronounced this last sentence caused a few of the meeker heads in the audience to bow or nod, almost involuntarily, in acquiescence.

"Think, finally, of all the unprotected and innocent trees that will now be spared the horrendous fate of ending their existence as ephemeral pages between covers. Think of all the oxygen that those trees will be able to produce for us and for those who come after us. Think how, soon, just because there will be no more books, you will claim back the ability to breathe freely, to fill your lungs!"

By way of example, the director took a deep breath,

then released it, surprising himself thereby with the immediate beneficial effect. It seemed to him he was in a field of violets. He had never realized auto-suggestion could be so persuasive.

"Last, but by no means least, we must mention the capacity of this unique storehouse of information. Although much smaller in size than an average book, it can absorb literally hundreds of volumes. Thousands, if they are not too large. An entire library can now fit quite literally in your pocket!"

With his free hand the director patted his empty pocket, large enough to hold a small encyclopedia. The purpose would have been better served if he had had a smaller pocket to pat but not everything can be arranged down to the last detail.

"No restrictions, no restraints any longer. Writers can now write as much as they wish. Not even the most prolific of them, not even the real graphomaniacs, will be able to fill a significant part of *one* of these in a single lifetime. What's more, the entire opus will reside in the same place. The dream of every author now comes true: to have his collected works published instantaneously.

"And the savings and benefits for the libraries! No longer will they have to throw away money on vast shelves, running wall to wall and floor to ceiling. All they will need will be one modest little shelf. So much easier to dust than a multitude of books all crammed together. And when you move house or apartment, a medium-sized bag will do to pack up the whole collection, not like now—countless cartons you have to drag and heave about—and books are, as we all know, as heavy as bronze.

"A man might almost wish for a disaster—fire, flood, or exile at the very least—just to enjoy the pleasure of such an easy and efficient move. Nothing would get ruined, nothing would get lost, as it always used to in the bad old days. The ancient proverb *Omnia mea mecum porto* would find its full expression. Life would continue quite smoothly in some other place, as though nothing at all had happened. What a joy."

The director stopped. He could go on about this topic for a long time yet, he had only just warmed to his theme. It filled him with zest, for it is no small thing to be the leader of a publishing revolution. But this heat was truly unbearable, he was drenched in perspiration, his shirt was sticking completely to his body, his jacket also was becoming damp. Couldn't anyone have repaired that accursed air-conditioning? Oh, well. There would be other opportunities and more auspicious circumstances; this was surely only the beginning. Some things, after all, had to be endured. *Per aspera ad astra!*

He slowly raised the hand containing the object he had recently taken from his pocket. Most of those gazes which were not yet wandering abstractedly about the room now fixed on the circular plaque flashing silvery reflections at them and producing occasional iridescent glints which covered the entire spectrum of the rainbow.

"Honored listeners, here at last is an invention which represents the guarantee of a new age in publishing! Here is the foundation on which we will build the magnificent edifice which will be the culture of this new millennium!"

He began waving his hand to and fro, so that everyone could get a good view of the glittery disk. As he did so, in a solemn hush, an extraordinary impression suddenly overwhelmed him: that he was not really here, in some crummy bookshop; that he had just descended from a tall mountain, and that he was now displaying to his compatriots a stone tablet bearing some inscription of immeasurable importance.

Understandably affected by his vision, he thundered in a deep prophetic voice:

"Ladies and gentlemen, the Book is dead—long live the CD ROM!"

# Afterword

by Zoran Živković

*THE BOOK* WAS CREATED during the first half of 1999. It was the time of the NATO campaign against my country. To a tragedy I responded with a comedy. Amidst death and destruction I was writing—whenever there was electricity to use my computer—a satire, occasionally hilarious. I imagine it was my vital reaction. Eros opposing Thanatos. *The Book* is still the funniest of all the 22 books of mine written so far.

As you know by now—if you are not reading this afterword as if it were a foreword—*The Book* is a novel about the last days of the Gutenberg era. It is narrated mostly by paper books themselves which are about to be replaced by their electronic successors.

In the closing years of the 20th century, however, it was still far too early for what the majority of us (conservatively enough—in accordance with my advanced age and out of my loyalty toward printed books—I don't belong to that progressive group) quite routinely use in 2016: e-books and various digital readers.

The state of the art computer technology back in 1999 was the CD-ROM. That's the reason I used it at the end of *The Book* as a symbol of the post-Gutenberg era. If I were to write my novel nowadays, I would feature the e-book, of course.

The rate of progress in this field is really astounding. The latest generation of my creative writing students, who, by coincidence, were born in 1999, probably have some vague idea what a CD-ROM is, but they have certainly never used it. For them, it is a relic from a much more primitive digital past. (Curiously enough, they still predominantly use even more primitive printed books. . . .)

You might wonder why I haven't updated *The Book* in the meantime. There have been many editions, in many countries, in the decade and a half since the original was published in 2000, in which I could have done it. The novel would certainly seem much more contemporary.

Indeed, there were some publishers who insisted on the finale of *The Book* being updated either by modifying it to replace the CD-ROM with the e-book or by adding another chapter. I persistently rejected these ultimatums even at the cost of not having my novel brought out.

I did so because, first of all, I wouldn't like there to be various versions of any of my books. Once they are originally published, they should remain unchanged in all subsequent editions in any language. Although I am often labeled by critics as a postmodern author, I am not so postmodern as to permit the confusion that would inevitably follow with multiple versions.

While this might also sound conservative, my other reason for refusing to update the end of *The Book* certainly isn't. On the contrary, it is very progressive. I firmly believe in the ever accelerating progress of computer technology. Even if I replaced the CD-ROM with e-books, it is quite possible that the new finale would be no more lasting than the original one.

Who could guarantee that in just a few years the e-book wouldn't become as obsolete as the CD-ROM is today? What should I do then? Write a new update of *The Book?* And continue to do so with every new phase in the digital revolution as long as I am around? I may be a postmodern author, but that would be a post-postmodernist experiment. If I agreed to participate in it, I would betray the very reason *The Book* was written in the first place. . . .

# Contributors

# About the author

**Zoran Živković** was born in Belgrade, Serbia, on October 5, 1948. Until his recent retirement, he was a full professor at the Faculty of Philology, the University of Belgrade, teaching creative writing. He is one of the most translated contemporary Serbian writers: by the end of 2019 there were more than 100 foreign editions of his books of fiction, published in 23 countries, in 20 languages.

Živković has won several literary awards for his fiction, beginning with the Miloš Crnjanski award in 1994 for his novel *The Fourth Circle*. In 2003, Živković's mosaic novel *The Library* won a World Fantasy Award for Best Novella; in 2007 his novel *The Bridge* won the Isidora Sekulić award; and in 2007 he received the Stefan Mitrov Ljubiša award for lifetime achievement in literature. In 2014 and 2015 he received three awards for his contribution to the literature of fantastika: Art-Anima, Stanislav Lem and The Golden Dragon.

Zoran Živković has been recognized with his selection as European Grand Master for 2017 by the European Science Fiction Society at the 39th Eurocon in Dortmund, Germany.

Živković is the author of 22 books of fiction:
    The Fourth Circle (1993)
    Time Gifts (1997)
    The Writer (1998)
    The Book (1999)
    Impossible Encounters (2000)
    Seven Touches of Music (2001)
    The Library (2002)
    Steps through the Mist (2003)
    Hidden Camera (2003)
    Compartments (2004)
    Four Stories till the End (2004)
    Twelve Collections and the Teashop (2005)
    The Bridge (2006)
    Miss Tamara, The Reader (2006),
    Amarcord (2007)
    The Last Book (2007)
    Escher's Loops (2008)
    The Ghostwriter (2009)
    The Five Wonders of the Danube (2011)
    The Grand Manuscript (2012)
    The Compendium of the Dead (2015)
    The Image Interpreter (2016)

# About the artist

**Youchan Ito** was born 1968 in Aichi prefecture, Japan. She launched her career as a graphic designer in 1988, becoming a freelancer illustrator in 1991 and founding Togoru Co., Ltd. with her husband in 2000. In 2017 the company was reborn as Togoru Art Works. She works with a wide range of genres including cover art and design for science fiction, mysteries and horror titles, as well as illustrations for children's books.

www.youchan.com